BLOOD BROTHERS

BLOOD BROTHERS

Marilyn Halvorson

Fitzhenry & Whiteside

Published in Canada by Fitzhenry & Whiteside, 195 Allstate Parkway, Markham, Ontario L3R 4T8

Published in the United States by Fitzhenry & Whiteside, 121 Harvard Avenue, Suite 2, Allston, Massachusetts 02134

godwit@fitzhenry.ca   **www.fitzhenry.ca**

10 9 8 7 6 5 4 3 2 1

Library and Archives Canada Cataloguing in Publication

Halvorson, Marilyn, 1948-
    Blood brothers / Marilyn Halvorson.

ISBN 1-55005-085-0

    I. Title.

PS8565.A462B59 2004   jC813'.54   C2004-903689-0

U.S. Publisher Cataloging-in-Publication Data (Library of Congress Standards)

Halvorson, Marilyn.
    Blood brothers / Marilyn Halvorson.–1st ed.
    [140] p. : cm.

Summary: Steve has been on the run from the law for so long that he barely remembers what it is to be normal. When he finds out his brother has leukemia and needs a bone marrow donor, Steve has no choice but to risk his freedom, and his life, by going home.

ISBN 1-55005-085-0 (pbk.)

1. Brothers—Fiction—Juvenile literature. 2. Cancer – Patients—Fiction — Juvenile literature. I. Title.
[Fic] dc22   PZ7.H358Bl   2004

Fitzhenry & Whiteside acknowledges with thanks the Canada Council for the Arts, the Government of Canada through the Book Publishing Industry Development Program (BPIDP), and the Ontario Arts Council for their support of our publishing program.

Book design: Fortunato Design Inc.
Cover image: Janet Wilson

Printed and bound in Canada

Acknowledgements

This book would not have been possible without a lot of help from numerous friends—and strangers—who allowed me to pick their brains for information from their fields of expertise. I would like to say thank you to the following people:

Keith, for some law-enforcement information
Tom, for the fishing information
Bill, for the "hot car" terminology
Beverly, Gwen, and Lori, for medical information—with which I know I took liberties to make the story work
Marilyn and Ken, for the quality control reading

*To Lynne (not the one in the book)
—a friend to count on whether wrestling
with calves or computers!*

Chapter 1

BUTTE, MONTANA IS A TOWN FULL OF GHOSTS. Ghosts of the old copper kings who got rich off the rock and built hillside mansions that outlived their owners. Ghosts of the men who lived and died sweating the ore out of the sunburned hills. And ghosts of the mines themselves, most of them gone into history with only slag heaps left behind for tombstones. I had a few ghosts of my own and sometimes on hot nights like tonight, when I couldn't sleep, I'd drive up the side of the butte that gave the town its name. Parked up high as those suicidal streets could take me, I'd sit there alone in the moonlight, listening to the radio and wondering how an Alberta kid who started out just wanting to be a cowboy like his dad ever messed up this bad.

This was one of those nights I'd had to work until after midnight, doing a rush job stripping a brand new Corvette. That was after a full day's work at The Cadillac Ranch Body Shop. But there wouldn't be any time and a half for overtime. Just like there wouldn't be any deductions for unemployment insurance or a pension plan or any of the stuff that ordinary people get on their paychecks. I didn't even get a paycheck. Just an envelope of cash every couple of weeks—and not that much cash. When you're in the country illegally you aren't about to complain.

One mistake, one little brush with the cops, and all they'd have to do would be to check my prints with the RCMP. I'd be getting an all-expenses-paid trip back to Canada—and to the prison where I'd walked away from day parole almost three years ago. And Al Davich, my boss at the body shop, knew it. That was one reason he kept me on the crew that did the "rush jobs." Those cars we stripped and repainted at night were hot—hotter than jalepeños—stolen in cities all across the west and filtered down to places like Al's for plastic surgery and new identities. As long as the guys who worked on them couldn't afford to get too talkative, Al figured he was safe.

I took a deep breath of the night air but all I could smell was paint. It was past 2:00 AM now and I was bone tired. I should go and get some sleep but I couldn't face that airless room over the rundown pool hall tonight. I closed my eyes and leaned my head against the cool glass of the side window. Maybe the radio would put me to sleep. It was tuned to a country station. Pretty strange for me—or at least for the guy who used to be me. My music was heavy metal and hard rock. The harder the better. But a few people I had known kind of wore me down until I started listening to their kind of music. Especially one girl. Lynne. As I thought of her my hand automatically reached inside my t-shirt to touch the little golden Camaro that hung on a chain around my neck. Lynne, the country girl who loved horses, hot cars, and—for some unexplainable reason—me. The charm wasn't much to make the loneliness go away, but right now it was all I had. Maybe all I was ever going to have.

For just a little while everything had been so right between us. So right that I actually started believing we could settle down and live happily ever after just like they do in the movies. Then, I told Lynne the truth about why I had to spend all my time looking over my shoulder. The next thing I knew, she was gone, leaving me nothing but a "Dear John" letter and the gold Camaro charm.

There was an old country song playing now. "I Miss Billy the Kid," it was called. About this guy remembering what it was like being little, pretending he was Billy the Kid. I knew what he was talking about. I'd been Billy the Kid, too. That was the nickname that Beau, my kid brother, gave me. I missed those days, too. Missed being little enough for your biggest problem to be getting home in time for supper—when the bad stuff in your world was mostly imaginary and you could ride in on your white horse and straighten it all out. Yeah, I missed Billy the Kid, too.

I smiled. Who was I trying to fool? I still *was* Billy the Kid. Wanted by the law. Enemies from the wrong side of the law on my trail, looking for a chance to kill me. I opened my eyes and looked down at my hands, rough and cracked and permanently paint-stained, souvenirs of my romantic outlaw lifestyle at the Cadillac Ranch Body Shop. Not gunfighter's hands.

I wasn't proud of working for a crook like Davich, and maybe I wouldn't have taken the job if I'd known I'd be working on hot cars. I've worked both sides of the street—straight and crooked—and lately I've liked straight a lot better. But sometimes you just fall into things. I fell into this job because the transmission fell out of my truck just outside of Butte. I limped into the first garage I could find. While I was waiting for the bad news on how much the repairs were going to cost, I wandered over next door to check out the lot full of half-restored old Caddies that gave the body shop its name. Al Davich himself happened to stroll out about then and we got talking about restoring old cars. I told him about the old Charger I'd fixed up and painted "Plum Crazy Purple", and when he found out I knew something about body shop work he offered me a job.

I said I'd think about it. Ten minutes later, when I found out the transmission was going to cost me about a thousand bucks more than I had, I'd thought about it enough. That was more than six months ago. For the first while Davich just kept me on the day crew, doing the legal stuff. It was after he found out I didn't have a green card—or any of the other papers I needed to even be in the country—that he introduced me to the real business of the Cadillac Ranch Body Shop. I'd been doing makeovers on hot cars ever since.

After I paid for a few luxuries, like eating and having a place to sleep, I was twenty-three dollars ahead right now. It looked like I'd be here for a while yet. But right now I was too tired to care. I closed my eyes and let myself drift….

Somebody was inside my head tapping on my skull. No, they were on the outside but it was real close. I struggled upward through an ocean of sleep. There was a click and suddenly the door I was leaning against was jerked open. Then I was wide-awake, sitting bolt upright with one hand locked on the shirt front of whoever had opened that door. In my other hand, my six-inch switchblade gleamed dully in the faint glow of a street-light. That same light caught the shocked eyes of big Leroy Sinclair.

I let out my breath in a long shaky sigh and loosened my grip on his shirt. "Leroy, don't ever sneak up on me like that again. You just took ten years off my life."

"Your life?" Leroy squawked. "I'm the one that just about got punctured with that toad-sticker of yours. Cool your jets, man! I got somethin' to show you."

I checked the time. A quarter to five in the morning—and Leroy wants to show me something. That didn't surprise me too much. Leroy was about six-foot-three and weighed over two hundred and fifty pounds, most of which was pure muscle. He looked like he'd be your worst nightmare if you met him in a dark alley, but he was as harmless as a twelve-year-old kid. Mentally, he pretty much *was* a twelve-year-old kid. He'd spent a lot of years as a boxer when he was younger, and I guess he'd been hit in the head a few too many times because now he had some trouble putting two and two together and coming up with four. He was good with cars, could drive anything, and Davich put all Leroy's muscle to good use, doing a lot of the heavy work at The Cadillac Ranch. Davich treated Leroy a little worse than he did me, always finding him one more chore to do, giving him all the dirtiest jobs. I'd seen the anger smolder in Leroy's cloudy eyes a few times when Davich had pushed him a little farther than usual, but I never saw Leroy stand up to him.

"Okay, Leroy," I said wearily as I switched on the dome light. "Climb in and let's see what you've got." He got in on the passenger side and pulled a crumpled-up piece of newspaper out of his pocket.

"Here, Steve, you better look at this. I found it when I was unpacking some new headlights this afternoon, but I didn't think anybody else should see it so I saved it till I could find you alone."

Still half-asleep I took the paper. It was a page from a Great Falls newspaper and, from the date at the top, it was a couple of weeks old. I looked at the picture, an ad for a shiny new Jeep with all the bells and whistles. Then I looked at Leroy. "Yeah?" I said, trying not too successfully to hang onto my patience, "It's nice, Leroy, but why did I need to see it in the middle of the night?"

He gave me a puzzled look, then grabbed the paper and turned it over. "*This* side, Steve." And there I was, staring back at us from the Personals. I hadn't spent a lot of time getting my picture taken lately, but back in Alberta I'd kind of accidentally saved a guy from drowning and was just unlucky enough to have an amateur newspaper photographer show up and snap my picture just as I was dragging him out of the river. This was that same picture but what it was doing in a Great Falls paper was a good question. And the one-line message under it just led to more questions.

Steve. Call home. Urgent. Life and Death. Pop.

Suddenly I was wide awake—and scared. Pop knew why I was hiding out down here but he didn't know exactly where. He also knew I didn't need to have my picture spread across half of Montana. For him to take the chance of putting this ad in the paper—something had to be wrong at home. Real wrong.

Leroy was studying my face. "Is this important, Steve? Did I do good to save it for you?"

"Yeah, Leroy, it's important. You did real good. I'll give you a ride home and then I have to go phone my dad."

Chapter 2

"HELLO?" It was Pop's unmistakable gravelly voice.

"Hi, Pop."

There was a long pause. "Steve?" The tone was almost unbelieving now. "It's really you?"

"Sure, Pop." I tried to keep the uneasiness out of my voice. "Why're you so surprised? Haven't you been advertising over half of Montana for me to call home?"

"Yeah, I have," Pop said, his voice suddenly sounding old and tired. "I put that ad in every paper in the western Border States. I'm sorry, Steve. I know publicity is the last thing you need but I didn't have any choice. I had to find you."

Before I could ask why, I heard another voice in the background. It sounded like Beau, my kid brother. "Pop, is that Steve?" Then, Beau's voice again, louder this time. "Don't tell him, Pop. Please don't tell him. If you do he'll come back. He can't afford to take the risk."

"He's got to know, Beau. He knows the risks and you've gotta give him the right to make his own choice."

"No, I'm not gonna let him!"

"Let go of the phone, Beau."

"Pop," I began, "what's—" but a loud click interrupted me. "Pop? Pop?" It was no use. The line was dead.

For a minute I just stood there, staring at the silent phone and wondering if I was losing my mind. Then I shook my head and started pushing buttons again. I heard the phone ringing on the other end—and ringing and ringing and ringing. I paced the length of the receiver cord. Come on, Pop, answer it. You were right there a minute ago, why don't you answer? And why did you hang up in the first place? Or was it even you that hung up? "Let go of the phone, Beau," was what Pop had said. And what was Beau yelling about not telling me? This whole thing was starting to freak me out.

Somebody picked up the phone. "Hello. Steve?" Pop again, but he sounded like he'd just run a mile. "Sorry about the interruption. Just had a little tussle with your brother."

"Pop," I said slowly, "what the hell is goin' on up there? And what did you mean about it being a matter of life and death?"

The line hung silent for a minute—except for Pop's heavy breathing. "I meant just that," he said, sounding old and tired again. "I don't know how to break this to you easy, so I might as well just come out and say it. Beau's got leukemia."

"What?" I whispered, even though I'd heard him loud and clear.

Leukemia was something people got in those sentimental Disease-of-the-Week TV movies. It happened to pale little kids and skinny housewives. It didn't happen to my pizza-eating, bronc-riding, football-loving eighteen-year-old brother.

"Steve? You there?"

I swallowed. "Yeah, I'm here, Pop. So, how's he doin'? Is he real sick now?"

"He's worse some times than others. He's pretty sick after he gets the chemo and he's tired all the time, but he's managing to keep up his schoolwork so he's hangin' in there..." He hesitated and then said, real quiet, "...for now."

"What d'you mean 'for now'?" The fear inside me came out as anger in my voice.

"Just what I said, Steve. Beau's gettin' worse. The doctor doesn't think the drugs are gonna do it."

"And if they don't?" It felt like a big, hard hand was squeezing my throat.

"He's got one other chance." Pop paused. "You."

"Me? What d'you mean?"

"Bone marrow transplant. Doc says it's got a chance of workin' if they find a perfect match. I've already been tested and it won't work. Siblings are the best bet they say. Full brother or sister's most likely to come up with a match."

"Okay, so what do I have to do?"

"Come up here for starters. Get tested. If you're a match they siphon some of this healthy stuff out of you and plant it in your brother."

I took a deep breath. "All right, Pop," I said. "I'll be there in a couple of days."

I heard Pop sigh with relief. But when he spoke again his voice was worried. "You better think this through, Steve. You're going to be putting yourself in a pretty vulnerable position going into the hospital and all. You'll be taking a chance."

He was right about that. Showing up back in Alberta and admitting that I was Beau Garrett's brother was a real good way to leave a trail for my old buddy, Carlos Romero. He'd already tried to kill me twice and I knew he'd like to try for strike three—if I didn't get picked up by the cops and sent back to British Columbia for breaking parole first. But right now none of that mattered. "Yeah, Pop, but at least I've got a chance to take. That could be more than Beau's got without me."

"Okay, Steve, I'll let the doctor know you're comin'."

"Pop?" I stopped him before he could hang up. "Let me talk to Beau."

Pop sighed. "I'll try, but I'm not sure he's speakin' to either one of us. Beau, Steve wants to talk to you," I heard in the background.

"Leave me alone." There was a long silence but I sensed that Beau had picked up the phone.

"Beau?"

"What?" His voice was angry and stubborn.

"Hey, Beauregard," I said softly, teasing him with the full name he hated. I tried to swallow the lump in my throat. "Sorry to hear you're sick, kid."

"Don't you 'kid' me, Steve." He sounded like he'd either been crying or was just about to start. "I'm sick of bein' treated like a kid. Where do you and Pop get off going ahead and making decisions as if my opinion doesn't even count? Well, I've got news for you. It's my life we're talkin' about."

"I know, Beau. That's why wild horses couldn't stop me from comin'."

Beau gave a disgusted snort. "You just don't get it, do you Steve? You know how dangerous it is for you to come back here. Romero came real close to killing you last time you came across the border, and there's no reason to think he won't try again. So

18

what if you make this big, gallant move and save my life—and you get killed for doin' it? You think I could live with that kind of guilt? You stay where you are. I might make it without the transplant. There's a couple of other things they can try. Besides, we might not even match. We sure never matched any other way." He finally ran out of breath.

"You finished, Beau?"

"Yeah, I'm finished." His voice was hard and I knew how he'd look right now—jaw set, eyes smoldering. Just the way he used to look when we were little and I'd made him mad enough to want to beat me up but he wasn't big enough to do it.

"Then shut up and listen long enough for me to ask you one question. Promise you'll tell me the truth?"

"Maybe."

"Not good enough."

"Okay, okay, I'll tell you the truth. What d'you wanna know so bad?"

"If things were reversed, would you come for me?"

When Beau swore at me I smiled. I knew I'd finally got through to him. He finally ran out of things to call me, and when he spoke again the anger was gone from his voice. "You know the answer to that," he said.

"Yeah, I know. See you in a few days."

Chapter 3

I DON'T KNOW HOW LONG I stood there with the receiver in my hand, staring into space and trying to take in what I'd just heard. It was one of those weird moments when something seems so unbelievable that you wish someone were there with you to prove you hadn't dreamed the whole thing. But I knew it was real, and when the phone started jabbering at me to hang up, I came back to reality. I was going home. Now. As fast as I could get there. How I was going to get across the border was another question. But I'd worry about that when I got there.

Right now I headed back to my room and packed. That took about three minutes. Everything I owned fit in one duffel bag. I left the key on the table with a note saying I wouldn't be back. Then I checked my wallet. Twenty-three bucks. That wouldn't buy much gas. But Davich owed me a couple of hundred. My next stop was the Cadillac Ranch. Even though daylight was starting to streak the eastern horizon I figured Davich would still be there. He'd just been getting into one of his regular all-night poker games in the backroom when I left at 1:00 AM.

I pulled up behind the shop. Davich's Caddy was there, along with a couple of other vehicles I recognized. The poker game was definitely on. I went over and banged on the door. Davich himself opened it. "What are you doin' here?" he growled. "Didn't you get enough hours of work last night?"

"Yeah, I had plenty of hours. And now I need to get paid for them. I'm leavin' town this morning."

"You're *what?*"

"You heard me. I just stopped to pick up my wages for last week."

A sly look crossed Davich's face. "What's the matter, Garrett? The law finally track you down?"

"This has nothin' to do with the law. It's personal. Just give me the money and I'm outta here."

"Uh-uh."

"What's that supposed to mean?"

"You ain't goin' nowhere today, Garrett. I've got a couple of Mustangs comin' in tonight to be stripped and I need you. Play your cards right and I might pay you off and let you go at the end of the week. Now get outta here and don't come back until opening time."

"I can't wait till the end of the week. I'm goin' now and I'm gettin' my money out of the cash drawer." I started toward the desk.

"Now, just a minute…" Davich was on his feet and coming up behind me. He grabbed me by the arm and spun me around to face him. My clenched fist came around to connect with his nose. He stumbled backward. "You dirty little…" It occurred to me that I'd been wanting to punch Al Davich for a long time now. Just once more and I'd get my money and walk away. But I should have run instead because right then Davich's poker pals decided to deal themselves in.

All two hundred pounds of Jake McGraw suddenly launched itself at me from behind. I landed right in the middle of the poker table with the wind knocked out of me. It crossed my mind that they'd never figure out who was winning now. Then McGraw grabbed my arms and pulled me upright just in time for me to collide with the fist of number three, Bob Hansen. Right about then I realized that I was about to get hurt. Or maybe killed. No, probably not killed. Dead bodies are nuisances to dispose of, and if they turn up somewhere the cops get real curious about how they got to be dead. Davich didn't need any curious cops nosing around The Cadillac Ranch. A good beating would get the message across, not only to me but also to anyone else who would see how sorry I was going to be that I'd crossed Davich. I gasped as Davich's big fist landed in the pit of my stomach. Yeah, I was sorry, all right, but not as sorry as he was going to be if I ever faced him one-on-one in a fair fight.

I don't know how many times I got hit. Keeping score isn't easy when you're on the edge of passing out. But I did notice that Davich was sticking mostly to body blows. I guessed that might have something to do with not attracting cops, too. He knew there was no way I'd dare to go anywhere near the police, but if my face looked too bad somebody else might get curious enough to ask some questions. So they just kept pounding away on my body, which hurt like hell, but I was glad they left my face alone. I'd always kind of liked it the way it was.

Suddenly, right in the middle of all the fun everybody but me was having, the door burst open. I was too busy trying to get my breath to look up but I recognized the voice instantly. Leroy. "Hey, what're you guys doin'?" Then I guess he took a look at me because he answered his own question. "Aw, come on! Stop that! What you wanna hurt Steve for? He never done nothin' to you."

Davich hesitated, fist in mid-air, and a surge of adrenaline rushed through me as I saw Leroy's huge hands clench into fists, too. All right! Leroy was gonna crack some heads. I struggled against the hands that held me. Go ahead, Leroy! Slug somebody! The two of us can take these guys easy.

But Leroy didn't slug anybody. He just stood there, frozen, staring at his own fist.

Davich gave a mocking laugh. "That's right, Leroy. You better think twice. You know what'll happen if you hit somebody. Now get outta here and pretend you don't know nothin'. That should come pretty natural to you."

I had enough wind back to yell, "Come on, Leroy! You don't have to take that. Go ahead and deck the—" McGraw gave my arm a vicious twist behind my back and the yell degenerated into a groan. Leroy's eyes met mine for a second with such a look of naked pain that it seemed like he was the one getting beat up. He looked at Davich, back down at his fist again, and then, with a sound almost like a sob, he turned and bolted out the door. Davich laughed again and drove his fist into my ribs so hard I barely bit back a scream. I quit struggling. I was out of strength, out of luck, and out of hope. Out of friends, too. The one guy I'd thought I could count on—big, tough Leroy—was yellow to the bone.

I slumped limply in McGraw's arms as another punch sent me drifting away on a wave of red-tinged pain. The red was getting black and peaceful around the edges. I was beyond feeling much more. Okay, guys, I don't care what you do 'cause I ain't sticking around at this party much longer....

But there was something important nagging at the tattered edges of my mind. Some reason I shouldn't be getting hurt. About half-conscious, I managed to force my eyes open and focus on Davich. "Hey," I whispered. "Just don't mess up my bone marrow." My eyes closed.

Dimly I heard Davich's voice, sounding confused. "Bone marrow? He's further gone than I thought. Better quit before he croaks on us."

The hands that were holding me suddenly let go. I remember falling but I was out cold before I landed.

Chapter 4

SNAKE. The thought filtered dimly through my returning-to-consciousness brain. Yeah, I thought, taking in the fact that my body was one big ache and remembering whose fault that was. Davich was a snake and McGraw was a snake and Hansen was a snake...and I was lying, sprawled on my back, looking into the beady eyes of a big, coiled rattlesnake. He was sitting about two feet from my face thoughtfully licking his lips or tasting the air—or doing whatever it is that snakes do with their little forked tongues.

For a few long seconds I completely gave up breathing. Then some calm corner of my brain suggested that it would probably be healthier to breathe normally than to wait until I had to take a great big snake-disturbing gulp of air. So I took a normal breath—normal except that it shook all the way in and all the way out again. The snake stayed cool so I got a chance to study the situation—as much as you can study anything when all you dare to move is your eyeballs.

I was out on the prairie somewhere. Besides the snake, my limited range of vision took in dry grass, sagebrush, a couple of rocks, and a huge blue bowl of cloudless sky with a fierce white sun burning its way toward high noon. I closed my eyes fast.

Looking at the sun usually makes me sneeze. I once heard about an old superstition that said your soul leaves your body for a second when you sneeze. I had a feeling if you sneezed this close to a rattlesnake your soul might leave for longer than that.

A minute later I risked another look. Snake was still just sitting there staring at me—or through me—with those unblinking eyes. Okay, Snake, you win the staring contest. I blinked, kept my eyes closed, and started silently counting. I'm not real good at sitting still at the best of times and I've always counted to keep from going crazy waiting for time to pass.

Every five hundred numbers I let myself sneak a peak at the snake. He was resting comfortably. I wasn't. Sweat was pouring off me as the climbing sun slowly turned the prairie into one big toaster oven. Hey, Snake, don't you know that the Health Department says being out here in all these ultraviolet rays is hazardous to the health? Probably not as hazardous as asking a coiled rattler to move.

Come on, Snake, you're a coldblooded animal, remember? Aren't you guys supposed to crawl under a rock when it gets hot? Stick around here and your blood's gonna boil. Good. Maybe you'll die. Or maybe you'll just get real irritable.

Six thousand and nine. Six thousand and ten. I was cheating. My eyes were open wide enough to catch a glimpse of movement. The snake had uncoiled. He was starting to slither. No, Stupid! Not *toward* me. Do I look like a rock to crawl under? Then I realized he wasn't actually heading in my direction; he just couldn't slither in a straight line. Maybe he was a sidewinder. Maybe he was getting sunstroke. Or maybe *I* was getting sunstroke. He made another sideways swoop and his tail slid over my outstretched hand, rattles clicking softly. In the broiling sun, I shivered. Then, the snake was gone from my line of sight.

I counted to another thousand before I got up the nerve to move. Then I wasn't so sure I *could* move. Davich and his goons had messed me up pretty good. I felt as twisted and rusted as the wrecks that sat outside the body shop. My spine was all seized up and my stomach muscles were screaming like guitar strings at a heavy metal concert. I wrapped an arm around my aching ribs, clenched my teeth, and managed to push myself off the ground with the other hand. Sitting up made me dizzy, but I shook my sweat-soaked hair out of my eyes and took a look around. I couldn't see much more sitting up than I had lying down, but I took in one important fact. The snake was gone. There was a pile of rocks a few feet away and I wondered if that was where he was hanging out. I didn't wonder enough to check it out, though.

I had other things to worry about. Like where I was. I listened to the silence. No traffic noise. No grumble of mine machinery. I was a long way from anywhere. Nobody out here but us snakes, I thought grimly as I dragged myself to my feet and stood swaying a little in the blazing sunlight.

Okay, so I could stand up. I took a step. Yeah, I could walk too, if I had to, but not too far. I wasn't crippled, just damaged some. I could see some of the bruises through my torn shirt. Real artistic. Why do they call it black and blue? I don't turn black and blue. Green and purple's more my style. Goes better with my blond hair maybe.

I ran a hand over my body. I hurt all over but probably nothing was broke. A cracked rib or two, maybe. My jaw was sore. I explored and found a loose tooth. Not so loose it wouldn't grow back, I hoped. Hang in there, baby. You and me definitely ain't goin' to the dentist anytime soon.

Even though it wasn't full summer yet, the heat was pounding down on me like a blacksmith's hammer and my mouth was so dry I couldn't even spit. If I was planning to get out of here alive I'd better start walking. But when you don't know where you are, it's real hard to know which way to go. Everything looked the same in all directions. But then something on the ground caught my eye. A tire track, barely noticeable on the hard-baked ground, but it was there all right. I bent down for a closer look, got dizzy, and almost fell on my face. I gave my head a shake, bent again—slowly this time—and started walking. There was a bent twig, an uprooted piece of sagebrush, a stone shifted from its hollow in the ground. Okay, now I knew how I'd got here. I could get out of here the same way. But it was going to be a whole lot harder on foot.

I walked for maybe an hour. It kept getting hotter. It was getting hard to walk in a straight line. I had to keep bending over to make sure I could still see the faint tire tracks, and every time I straightened up I got dizzy. Finally I got too dizzy to straighten up at all. There was a big rock a couple of steps away. I staggered over to it, sank down against it, and closed my eyes.

It was the sound of a motor that woke me up again. The sun was higher. I was still dizzy but when I focused my eyes I saw a truck coming toward me. My truck. My faithful Ford. It had come looking for me. Oh, no, I guess that's just horses in old movies that do that. But it *was* my truck. I closed my eyes again and leaned back against the rock.

Then, someone was shaking me and talking to me. "Wake

28

up, Steve. You gotta wake up. You gotta be okay. Please be okay, Steve."

Leroy. I took one look at him and turned away in disgust. Where were you when I needed you Leroy? I thought. You muscle-bound, yellow-bellied liar. Contender for the title? Yeah, right, Leroy. Maybe the title in the 100-meter run.

"Don't be mad, Steve. I came lookin' for you as soon as I could get your truck without gettin' caught. Are you all right? Did they hurt you bad?"

"You're a little late worryin' about it, aren't you, Leroy?" I muttered through my cracked lips. "Why'd you tell me that big lie about bein' a heavyweight contender?"

I shifted my head enough to meet his eyes. "You're scared of your own shadow, Leroy."

He flinched as if I'd hit him, which I might have done if I'd had the energy, but then a spark of anger lit somewhere in the depths of his cloudy eyes. "No way, Steve. That sure wasn't a lie. I could have taken all those guys."

"Yeah? So you just didn't think it was worthwhile skinnin' your knuckles on 'em?"

Leroy didn't answer for a minute. He just raised his big right hand and stared at it like it was some kind of horrible alien that had attached itself to his body. "I can't fight no more, Steve. Not ever," he said in a low, distant voice like he was talking more to himself than to me. "I killed a guy with this fist once.

"It was in Texas. I was with Davich. He was my manager then. We were outside a bar when this drunk came up and started taunt-ing me, calling me names and stuff. So I hit him. I only hit him once, Steve, honest. But he didn't get up. And I couldn't see him breathin'. I was so scared I didn't know what to do. I wanted to call 911 but Davich said not to. Nobody else saw what happened so he said we just had to get outta there. He said that a fighter's hands were like dangerous weapons and they'd put me in the gas chamber. He said that if I stuck with him he'd look after me. Make sure they didn't get me. So I've been with him ever since." His eyes met mine for the first time and I could see the tears. "I'm sorry I let you down, Steve. Please don't be mad."

Yeah, I thought. Davich has been looking after you, all right. He's had you for his own personal slave, doing all his dirty work and scared to cross him.

Right then I realized that Leroy was beat up a lot worse than I was. Only his scars were on the inside where they didn't show—and they didn't heal either. I dragged myself upright and threw an arm around his shoulders to make sure I stayed that way. "It's okay, Leroy, you done good. I'm not mad. Just take me home," I added, dragging myself into the passenger seat.

"Sure, Steve. I can do that." He started the truck and I leaned against the window and let myself drift—as much as you can drift bouncing across the prairie with a few hundred bruises and a truck that doesn't know the meaning of the words "shock absorber".

Leroy finally broke the silence. "Steve?"

"Mmm?"

"Where, exactly, did you mean by 'home'?"

"It's a long story. Just drive us back to town for now."

Chapter 5

I WOKE UP ALONE IN THE TRUCK. It was parked outside a 7-Eleven on the edge of town. Leroy was nowhere in sight. I was so thirsty I was about to croak, so I figured I'd buy myself a drink first and think about finding Leroy second. I unfolded myself from my slumped position and regretted the move. Nothing like a little time to make sore muscles ache a little more. I dug in my pocket and was relieved to find my wallet still there. Then I looked inside it and was a little less relieved. Davich and his boys had helped themselves to my twenty bucks. Now, I was down to—I checked my pockets for change—two dollars and thirty-nine cents. That wasn't going to do a lot toward getting me back to Alberta. But it *would* buy me a Coke.

I was just about to open the door when Leroy came out of the store with a big bag of stuff. "Hey, Steve, you woke up!"

"Yeah, more or less," I muttered. "What's in the bag?"

"Everything we need," he said, beginning to arrange it all on the seat. Apparently we needed a whole lot of licorice, beef jerky, and taco chips. But Leroy had also come up with a case of ice-cold Coke. We definitely needed that. I drank three cans before my throat stopped feeling like sandpaper.

"Thanks, Leroy. I'll help you pay for this later. Right now I've only got a little over two bucks."

Leroy grinned. "You've got a lot more than that," he said.

"What?"

He reached under the seat and brought out a brown envelope. He handed it to me. "When I went to get your truck I snuck in and took a look around the office. I found this envelope with your pay for the week in it." He brought out another envelope. "Found mine, too." Then a worried look crossed his face. "It wasn't stealin', was it, Steve? Since we'd already earned it and everything?"

I laughed. "No. It definitely wasn't stealing. We earned every cent. You done good, Leroy." I gave him a high-five and helped myself to a chunk of jerky. Chewing on it didn't do my loose tooth any good, which reminded me of what I *did* owe Davich.

"Back in a minute," I said, digging out my handful of change and easing my aching bones out of the truck.

"Where you goin'?"

"Just to pay a little debt."

"Must be real little if that's all the money you're takin'," I heard Leroy mutter as I closed the door. I grinned. It wasn't all that little but I had money enough. I headed for the pay phone.

"Butte City Police. How can I help you?"

"Actually, I think I can help you. There's a body shop on the west end of town called The Cadillac Ranch. If you send some-body to drop in there sometime after midnight you might find their after hours business a lot more interesting than their day work."

The voice that had answered the phone was suddenly replaced by one that sounded older and a lot more world-weary.

"All right, let's hear this again. What did you say your name was?"

"I didn't say. Just think of me as a passing stranger."

"I see. And what might the nature of this 'interesting work' be at this Cadillac Ranch place?"

"Figure it out. What do crooked body shops do best?"

"You mean they're running a chop shop?"

"Bingo."

"And how do you happen to be in possession of this information?"

"I used to work there. Boss's name is Al Davich and he's been workin' on hot cars for a long time. I've worked on them for him since last fall."

"Uh-huh. And what burst of civic responsibility has led you to report your boss to the police?"

"Let's just say that when my employment was terminated his crew did some unsatisfactory work on my chassis."

The cop gave a snort that might have been laughter. "Okay, Mr. Stranger. We'll have a little visit with Mr. Davich. Try to find yourself a better line of work."

"Yeah, I'll do that. And tell Davich I said hello. He won't need a name."

I hung up and headed back to the truck. Leroy turned to me with a worried look as I got in. "Steve, I been thinkin'," he said, real serious. "I guess maybe I better not go back to the shop either, now that I took that money, huh?"

I laughed, which was a bad idea because it made my stomach muscles hurt worse. I was still feeling pretty lousy all over but what I'd just done to Davich had cheered me up a lot. "No, I guess not. Drive over to your place and get your stuff, then let's blow this town. Wake me up at Great Falls."

I slumped down in the closest position to comfortable that I could find and thought about what I'd just done. This was the second crooked boss I'd double-crossed after they'd double-crossed me. Carlos Romero was the first, and he was still after me. He'd already tried to kill me more than once. But I didn't regret turning him in. I just regretted that his high-priced lawyer got him off on a technicality.

I didn't regret turning Davich in either. He didn't scare me any. Compared to Romero, Davich was just a puppy. And I figured that around midnight he was going to be one sick puppy.

Chapter 6

LEROY DIDN'T HAVE TO WAKE ME. I woke up on my own somewhere around Wolf Creek and dug my tattered old road map out from behind the seat. Now that Butte was history I needed to start figuring out what would come next. One thing was for sure; I wasn't going to just drive into Canada. I'd stopped being Steve Garrett a couple of years ago when I had to throw Romero off my trail. And now I wasn't anybody—officially, anyhow. I'd picked a couple of last names out of thin air when I needed them but I didn't have any papers. By working for a crook and driving like a grandma I'd managed to avoid the need to produce any ID since I'd been in Montana. But crossing an international border was a different story.

The truth is that I'd actually been across the border three times without any papers. The first time I didn't have any problem at all—about my papers that is. The rest of that little adventure nearly killed me. I'd got cornered in Waterton Park with Romero hot on my trail so I jumped on the tour boat that takes you to the Montana end of the lake and then just disappeared into the bush. The plan was to hike up to Going-to-the-Sun Highway and get a ride there. Well, the plan worked. I got there but I came so close to starving and freezing to death that it scares me to remember it. And I think I'd rather face any border guard than that bad tempered Ma Grizzly who beat me up and stole my lunch.

The next time I crossed was back into Alberta with a liner full of thoroughbreds and a chuck wagon on the trailer behind the pickup. I was taking them to the Calgary Stampede to race for Reece Kelly, the guy who'd given me a job, a place to live, and a life for almost a year. With all the commotion about checking the horses for vaccinations and everything, the border guys weren't too worried about the people. Reece had crossed enough times that they knew he was okay. At the end of the Stampede I went back to Montana—alone and fast. Yeah, Romero again. But I got lucky and was checked through by the same guy who'd watched us go through into Alberta ten days earlier, so he didn't make things too tough for me. But all that was before September 11, 2001. It was a whole new ball game now, and even though I didn't look much like your typical terrorist I was still going to need some paperwork to prove I even existed. Unless...

I looked at the map again. If we kept going toward Great Falls we'd end up at the Sweetgrass crossing, which was a main one between Montana and Alberta. We'd never get away with going through there. But if we cut off and headed up through Browning, we'd hit the border just on the edge of Glacier Park. That was wild country, nothing but a big blank square on the map. I was getting an idea.

"When you see the turnoff for Highway 287, take it, Leroy."

"Sure thing," he said, never questioning if I knew what I was doing. I was questioning it plenty. What I had in mind was seriously illegal and if I messed up I'd be in big trouble. So what else was new? But I didn't need to drag Leroy down with me.

"You got some family somewhere, Leroy?"

His eyes lit up. "Sure I do. My pa died in an accident when I was just little and my brother got himself killed in Vietnam, but my momma's still goin' strong. She works in a little cafe back in Spokane where I grew up. I call her up once in a while just to let her know I'm okay. Davich would be mad if he knew, but Momma worries about me when she don't hear from me."

"You don't have to worry about Davich anymore. He's not gonna bother you. Why don't you go home and take care of your mom?"

Leroy's face clouded. "I can't, Steve. I killed that guy. The police'll be lookin' for me. Davich said—" He caught himself. "Oh, yeah, Davich don't matter anymore, but—"

I had a headache and my patience was running thin. "Leroy," I said, "you don't even know for sure that guy is dead and even if he is, it was an accident. That was a long time ago and a long way away. I seriously doubt that anybody's lookin' for you. And I sure doubt they'd be lookin' for you in Spokane. And even if they caught you and locked you up, it wouldn't be forever. It would be worth the risk to be back with your mom and havin' a real life again. Hidin' out and never seein' your family until maybe it's too late is just plain stupid." I ran out of breath and shut up.

Leroy gave me a thoughtful look. "Hey, man," he said. "You preachin' to me or to yourself?"

And this was the guy who I thought was a little slow? Maybe it was about time to level with Leroy. "Myself mostly, I guess. I never told you the reason I needed to head back to Alberta so fast. Pop has been putting ads in the paper to find me because my brother might die. He's got leukemia and maybe a bone marrow transplant from me can save him."

Leroy thought on that for a while and I wondered if he even understood what I was talking about. But when he started talking again I realized he understood all too well. "Aw, Steve, that's awful," he said, his voice sounding choked. "You can't lose your brother. When my brother died in Vietnam it was like my whole world got a huge hole in it that nothin' would fill. You never get over losin' your brother."

I sucked in a deep breath and turned away to stare out the window for a long minute before I could answer. "I'm not gonna lose him," I said through clenched teeth.

There was nothing more to say. We drove in silence for a long time. On the outskirts of Browning we pulled in to a gas station. We filled the tank, made a pit stop, and grabbed a gourmet greasy burger—after a diet of licorice and jerky, gourmet wasn't hard to achieve. There was a pay phone by the door, and as we passed it I stopped Leroy. "Call your mom."

"Now? What am I gonna talk to my mom about right now?"

"You're gonna tell her to wait up for you 'cause you'll be home late tonight."

"What?"

I pulled out the map and drew a line with my finger. "Okay, here's how it's gonna work. You drive me up here past this little place called Babb. Then, you head back here, get on Highway 2 and follow it west till you hit Spokane and find your mom."

Leroy was shaking his head. "No, I can't—" He stopped short. "Where you gonna be?"

I grinned. "I'm gonna take a little hike through the woods, and if I'm lucky when I come out, I'll be in Alberta."

"Aw, Steve, I can't take your truck and leave you on foot."

"Yeah, you can. You have to. I'll never get away with driving through any of the border checkpoints, but there's miles of wild country out there with nobody but the moose and grizz keepin' track of who's passin' through. If I'm gettin' into Canada it'll have to be on foot. After that I can hitch a ride home."

Leroy shook his head again. "I don't know about goin' back to Spokane, Steve. I don't want to bring my mom any trouble."

I was getting tired of fighting this battle. "Leroy," I said, looking him straight in the eye. "Remember how you told me how bad it hurt to lose your brother?"

He nodded and I heard him swallow hard. "Well," I said, deliberately keeping my voice hard and accusing, "you think your mom's gonna live forever?"

"No," he said, in a choked voice, looking down to hide the tears in his eyes.

"That's right, Leroy. Life is real short and I don't want you to wake up some day and realize it's too late to go back and re-live all the years you didn't spend with her. So go make the call. I'll even pay." I dumped a bunch of change into his hand. He hesitated for a second and then headed for the phone.

I got in the truck and waited. In a few minutes he came striding back like a man who was going somewhere. "Well," I asked, "what'd she say?"

A huge grin spread over Leroy's face. "She said, 'Boy, you get in that truck and start drivin' and don't you stop for hell or high water till you get home.' Oh, yeah, and then she added, 'And don't you go pickin' up no speedin' tickets neither.' Ain't that just like a mom, Steve?"

I managed a grin. "Yeah, Leroy, I guess it is." And guess was the truth as far as I was concerned. I hadn't seen my mom since she took off when I was ten. I don't recall her throwing any words of wisdom back over her shoulder either.

We headed north. Less than an hour later we were on an empty stretch of road with nothing but hills and trees on either side. Off to the west, a sliver of the St. Mary's River gleamed through the openings between the trees. I figured we were within walking distance of the border. "Okay, Leroy, this is it. Pull over."

I got out of the truck and hauled my duffel bag out of the back. Leroy got out too and stood unhappily watching me. I could see him getting ready to back out of this deal if I gave him enough time, so I held out my hand. "Good luck, Leroy. Tell your mom I said hello."

He ignored my hand and grabbed me in a hug that would have put your average grizzly bear to shame and came close to killing me, as sore as I already was. "I'm gonna miss you, Steve. You're the best friend I ever had," he said, his voice going kind of husky. "Momma said she was prayin' for your brother."

I nodded and swallowed hard. "That's good. He needs all the help he can get." I broke away from him. "Now, go on, get outta here. And stay outta trouble."

Leroy gave me a sassy grin. "*You* are tellin' *me* to stay outta trouble? Which one of us was stuck out in the desert talkin' to the snakes just this mornin'?"

I laughed. Leroy was going to be okay. "You got it straight which way you need to go?"

"Yeah, I got it. I won't get lost. How 'bout you?"

"I'm cool," I said with a little more confidence than I felt. "Let's get goin'. We're burnin' daylight." I turned and walked off into the brush in what I hoped was the right general direction. After what seemed like a long time I heard the motor start and gravel crunch as the truck turned around. But I didn't look back.

Chapter 7

I WAS STILL WALKING WHEN it started to get dark and I was pretty well lost. Not so lost I didn't know that I was going north. I'd crossed what passed for the border a couple of hours ago. It didn't really look like a border, just a cleared strip that could have been one of the cut lines seismic companies make all over the country when they're looking for oil. I'd heard that in some places in British Columbia where there's a lot of drug traffic over the line they've put in motion sensors to catch anybody who tries to slip across. I took a careful look here but I didn't see anything more high tech than a pile of elk turds. I figured if they checked every moving thing that went through here, somebody would spend a lot of time trying to arrest the wildlife. So I just pretended I was a bear and walked right across. Nothing beeped, shrieked, or blew up. I was back in Alberta.

But aside from that, I didn't have a clue where I was. And right now I didn't much care. All the places I'd been punched were aching, my feet hurt from walking for about three hours, my greasy burger had worn thin, and I was back to gnawing on licorice and beef jerky. Having been awake almost all of last night didn't help much either so I was almost dead on my feet when I finally gave up and crawled under a tree for the night.

I thought I was tired enough to fall asleep right away but I didn't. I thought about Leroy and wondered if he'd get to his mom's place okay. If he got in any trouble it would be my fault for talking him into going. One more chunk of guilt to carry around. One more person I'd let down. That made me start thinking about Pop and Beau. Beau. It still seemed like I'd imagined the whole thing about him having leukemia. Maybe I'd wake up in the morning and find myself back in my truck, high up on the streets of Butte, and everything that happened since I fell asleep there would have been a dream. I shifted position, trying to get comfortable. Ouch. No, I was too sore to have imagined my run-in with Davich and his merry men. That was real, and the fact that Beau might die was real, too. Thinking about that, I came closer to crying myself to sleep that night than I had since Tracey, the first girl I ever loved, died in Vancouver.

I don't know how much later it was when I was suddenly awake again. It was pitch dark. There were about a million stars in the sky but there was no moon. That's why I couldn't see what it was that had woken me up. I could *feel* it, though. Well, actually it was its breath I could feel, hot and moist on my face. A few thousand volts of adrenaline shot through me and the first thought that went through my head was BEAR! If I'd figured it right, I should be just on the east side of Waterton-Glacier Park where I'd had that unpleasant encounter with Ma Grizz a couple of years back. I'd beat the odds and got away that time, but if I was a cat I'd be on life number nine about now. Every nerve in my body was hollering, "Run!" but my brain was fighting back with, "Don't move!" So far, my muscles were siding with my brain so I lay there frozen while the breathing—no, it wasn't just breathing, it was more like sniffing—moved across my face. Trying to decide if I'd make a satisfactory meal? I wondered.

I took a deep, shaky breath—and inhaled the smell of the critter. The old grizzly's breath had smelled awful. What can you expect of somebody whose favorite food is rotting carcasses? But this one didn't smell that bad. Kind of like warm grass—the kind horses eat, not the kind you smoke. It was a real familiar smell, but at that moment I couldn't quite place it. For some reason it took me back to the days when I when I worked on the Double C ranch, looking after a herd of cows.

Cows! Suddenly I sat bolt upright. There was a startled bawl and I narrowly missed getting stepped on as a huge critter with long shiny horns that gleamed dully in the starlight did an awkward pirouette and jumped backward, just as scared of me as I had been of it. Being very close to directly underneath this cow gave me one more piece of information. This cow was no cow. This was Mister Bull himself who'd been giving me the once over and asking himself "Who's this sleeping in *my* bed?" Fortunately this guy must have been hired as a lover not a fighter because, after his original panic, he forgot all about me and went back to stuffing himself with grass.

While I sat there waiting for my heart rate to return to something close to normal I could see the eastern sky beginning to lighten a little and the blackness around me easing into shades of gray. I started to notice big dark shapes all over the place and realized I was surrounded by grazing cattle. All right! If I was in the middle of somebody's grazing lease they must have brought the cattle in from some kind of a road.

I dug in my duffel bag and found myself a nutritious breakfast of jerky and lukewarm Coke. By daylight I was walking
again, following a well-beaten cow trail.

A few minutes later I came to a little gravel-bottomed mountain stream where the cows had been drinking. Despite that fact,
the water looked cold and clear and so much more thirst quench-
ing than warm Coke that I went upstream a ways, laid down on
my belly and had a good long drink. If I could survive Davich
and his boys and my friend Snake, I didn't think beaver fever was
likely to kill me.

I crossed the creek and kept following the well-beaten cattle
trail. It led to a trampled opening where a couple of blocks of
blue cow salt had been put out. Those things weighed fifty
pounds apiece so I didn't figure anybody had walked in with
them. Sure enough, there were quad tracks going out of the other
side of the clearing. I followed them for maybe an hour as the
country started opening up into more meadows dotted with
clumps of trees. Over my left shoulder the face of Chief
Mountain brooded down at me. Right where it should be. I was
still headed north—and home.

The quad trail came out at a gate that led to a gravel road.
Half an hour of walking on it brought me to an intersection with
a paved road. Highway 6, a sign said. A little ways farther on,
another sign said Pincher Creek 50 km. I was definitely headed
in the right direction. The next question was how far was I from
the border? Would I be unlucky enough to cross paths with some
cop or dutiful citizen who thought I looked kind of suspicious out
here in the middle of nowhere on foot and carrying a duffel bag?
Okay, I could solve half of that. I rescued my jacket, my last can

of Coke, and a big handful of licorice. Then I tossed the bag into the bushes. Maybe a cold cougar would find it and get some use out of a couple of t-shirts and my holey underwear.

Chapter 8

I CAUGHT SIGHT OF A CAR topping a ridge behind me. No, at that distance I couldn't be sure it wasn't a cop car, and if I waited to be sure, it would be too late to disappear. I melted into the brush and watched a white Buick with two gray-haired women in it sail by with a soft swish. Okay, so maybe they weren't dangerous but they could have been curious types. I walked on.

There wasn't a whole lot of traffic on this road. When another vehicle finally showed up on the horizon I was feeling a whole lot less choosy. Besides, it was a half-ton pulling a horse trailer. Horse people are usually okay. They have more important things on their minds than looking for a way to mess somebody up. I stepped onto the edge of the road and stuck out my thumb.

The truck slowed down—not that it was going very fast in the first place. Probably *couldn't* go very fast in the second place. It was a Chevy from back in the days when trucks still had style, maybe about a seventy-nine or eighty, and carrying a fair bit of rust. The two-horse trailer looked just as old and twice as rusty.

I waited to see who might be driving a rig like this. I've got tangled up with some pretty scary people while I've been hitching and I like to look them over before I get in. The truck rolled to a stop and the driver stuck his head out. Speaking of scary people...

He had on a greasy old Stetson that wasn't having any luck keeping his hair in captivity. The hair was red with enough gray mixed in to make it about the color of a strawberry roan horse. Wiry curls of it shot out under the edges of the hat and sproinged out in all directions and a pair of sharp blue eyes had all they could do to peer out from the forest of wild red and gray whiskers that covered most of his face.

"Howdy there, partner. I reckon y'all must be lookin' for a ride."

Yeah, I thought, when did you get your first clue? Maybe the fact I had my thumb out gave it all away. I had to make a fast decision on whether I wanted to get in with this guy. I took a glance through the opening in the side of the trailer. The horse was a bay, sleek and in good shape, calmly munching a little hay from the net that hung in front of him.

"Yeah," I said, "I sure could use a ride." About the surest way I ever found to judge people was by how they treated their animals. This guy's horse said he was okay, so I walked around to the passenger side and climbed in.

"Thanks for stopping," I said. "I was gettin' real tired of walkin'."

Those sharp eyes gave me the once-over as he put the truck in gear and eased out the clutch. "Yeah, reckon you do look a little the worse for wear. Been on the road long?"

Oh great. He was going to be the curious type. "Oh, a few days," I said vaguely.

Wrong answer. Another thoughtful glance. "Travelin' kinda light, ain't ya?"

And I'd thought dumping the duffel was such a brilliant idea. I considered making up some kind of story about how my luggage was lost, strayed, or stolen, but I was just too tired to be creative so I didn't say anything. That didn't help either. The guy stroked his whiskers thoughtfully. "Not far to the border back there," he said.

I didn't say anything.

"Can't hardly figure where you could be hiking from in this direction for a few days without crossing it." I still didn't say anything and he finally got to where he was going with this conversation. "I'm kinda thinkin' maybe you did cross it but you just skipped the formalities. Maybe just cut across country?" He shot me another of those piercing looks and my hand strayed toward the door handle.

All of a sudden he burst out with a bellow of laughter so loud I actually jumped. "Hey, kid, don't get your shorts in a knot. I ain't the border patrol. It don't matter to me how you got here. I'm just impressed that somebody your age would walk far enough to pull it off. Most of the young fellas I run across these days are too dog-lazy to get up and turn off the TV so they can turn on the radio." He stuck out his hand. "I'm Archie McCrae. Me an' ol' Jimbo back behind us there have got a trick horse and clown act we do at some of the small-time rodeos on both sides of the border." We shook hands. Then he looked over at me again. "You need a name, too, you know. It don't have to be your real one but I don't want to call you Hey You all the time you ride with me."

I'd relaxed enough to return his grin. "Steve Garrett," I said, with only a little hesitation in between. Somehow the idea that he expected me to lie was just enough to make me tell him the truth. "And," I added, a little defiance creeping into my voice, "it *is* my real name."

Archie shrugged. "Good a name as any, Steve. Where you headed?"

"Fenton. You ever heard of it?"

"Sure. I'm headed for Water Valley. Fenton's only another half-hour or so."

"Great. You live in Water Valley?"

"Just outside it, when I'm home. My lady holds down the fort when I'm away. She'll be expectin' me today. I'll pull in and unload ol' Jimbo and give him a feed of oats, and then Molly'll have roast beef and apple pie waitin'—"

"You're beginning to sound like an Ian Tyson song," I interrupted.

That didn't discourage Archie. "Say, did I happen to mention I'm a singer, too?" Without waiting for a reply he broke into a verse of "On the Road Again."

Actually he wasn't too bad, but by the time he'd moved into his fourth number I'd had enough entertainment for a while. I dug in my pocket, found the last of my licorice and held out a stick. He accepted and before he could chew, swallow, and sing again, I'd slumped down and fallen asleep.

I must have slept for quite awhile because, when I woke up, we were stopped at a red light and the windshield wipers were softly swishing through a light rain. "Where are we?" I mumbled, trying to work the kink out of my neck.

"Just on the edge of Cochrane," Archie said, shaking his head. "The way this place is spreadin' out, it'll soon meet

Calgary. Alberta's gettin' way too civilized."

I agreed with him but I didn't say anything because it had suddenly hit me that I was only about an hour from home now. Home? That's what I'd called it in my head. I'd only spent a few weeks there a couple of years ago. Why was I thinking of it as home? Then I remembered a line I'd read somewhere. "Home is where they have to take you in." Yeah, that was it. As long as I knew Pop and Beau were there I had roots. I might never go home but it was there. *They* were there—for now, at least. But what if I lost Beau? Suddenly, I wanted to grab the wheel from ol' Archie and put the pedal to the metal. I had to get home *now*. But at the same time I didn't want to get there at all. A voice in my head laid it on the line for me. You're scared, Steve. You've finally run into something you can't outrun and you can't out-fight. You're gonna have to grow up and face it. I told the voice to shut up and concentrated on the scenery.

We reached the Water Valley turnoff. Archie pulled over. He looked out at the steadily falling rain. "You're gonna get wet if you start walkin' here," he said. "Why don't you come home with me for the night? Molly'll throw in another spud and you can start again in the morning."

I shook my head. "Thanks, Archie, but I've got to get home now."

He nodded. "Figured you were gonna say that. I don't know what's goin' on with you, but from the way you were talkin' in your sleep a ways back there you've got something on your mind." His gaze softened a little. "Good luck, then, Steve. I hope it all works out for you." He gave me another of his bruising handshakes and I stepped out into the rain.

I started walking. It was raining a little harder. An occasional flash of lightning lit up the sky and thunder rumbled steadily in the west. A few cars swished by, throwing up enough water to soak any parts of me that the rain had neglected. Nobody even slowed down. I was beginning to doubt that I would make it home tonight. Then a Volkswagen bug went by. Its brake lights flashed and then the backup lights came on. I had a winner.

But when the car pulled up beside me and I went to open the passenger door it was locked. The window slid down and the woman behind the wheel leaned toward me. "Come over to this side. I need to see you before I let you in." I sloshed over and, just as she stuck her head out the driver's side, a really impressive flash of lightning lit the whole countryside like an out-of-control strobe light. There you go, lady, I thought. If you saw me any better than that I'd be vaporized.

"Wow. That was close," she said calmly, not about to let a few million volts of electricity hurry her decision. "My son would never let me hear the end of it if he knew I picked up a hitchhiker," she said, mainly to herself. "He thinks I take far too many chances for a woman of my age. I'm 65, you know." I didn't know. She actually looked a little younger. But I cared even less.

"Ma'am," I said, dredging up every ounce of politeness I'd ever owned. "I really need a ride and—not that you've got any reason to believe me—I'm not dangerous. But if you aren't going to give me a ride could we stop discussing it here on the top of this hill? I didn't learn much in school, but one thing I remember is that lightning usually strikes the highest object. Right now, that would be me."

She burst out laughing. "I'm glad you at least learned *some-*

thing in school. That's probably more than I could say for some of my students when I was teaching." There was a click as she hit the unlock button. "Get in quick."

I got in, dripping water all over her seat covers. "Sorry I'm so wet," I said, trying unsuccessfully to keep my teeth from chattering.

"Me too," she said, and turned the heater on high. "Where are you going?" I told her. "Well, you're in luck. I go right by Fenton. And I'm in luck because I'll get you out of here before my son happens to catch me with another of my 'derelict friends' as he calls the people I'm forever trying to help out."

"Your son sounds like a lot of fun."

"Oh, he's not so bad. He's just the cautious type, always look-ing out for dear old Mom in case I'm getting senile. Anyhow, I just tell him that my derelict friends tell me where all the best fishing holes are. That shuts him up for a while."

She talked some more about nothing in particular and I answered when it seemed necessary, and before I knew it we were at the Fenton turnoff. "Are you right in town?" she asked. "I can run you right to where you're going so you don't have to get wet again."

I laughed. "No, that's okay. Aside from what soaked into your car seat, I never got over being wet the first time. Anyhow, I need a few minutes to think. Thanks for the ride." Then I remembered something I'd heard the last time I was in Fenton. "Oh, yeah," I added, "I hear they're catching some decent brown trout in the Fallen Timber south of Bergen."

She laughed and drove off into the rainy night.

Chapter 9

THERE WAS A LONG HILL outside Fenton and it seemed to take forever to slog up it in the rain. But at last I was there, looking right down at Pop's place below. I was relieved to see that nothing had changed. The same white, two-story house that still needed painting. The little shop where Pop did his saddle-making, the old barn, and a single-car garage that was probably still full of junk because Pop's old half-ton was sitting out in the rain. Hey, something had changed. A shiny gray and black Chevy was sitting out there, too. The truck was probably nearly old enough to have its own driver's license but it had the look of a lot of TLC about it. Beau's truck, I figured. And that, like every other thought I had about my brother, made me swallow hard to get rid of the lump in my throat.

All of a sudden the thought of actually walking up to the house scared me half to death. I'd nearly got myself killed to get here but now I wasn't sure I could handle seeing my brother. But I didn't have a choice.

A minute later I was standing on the back step banging on the door. I remembered the last time we'd met like this—Beau opening the door to find his long-lost brother standing there. It had been raining then, too, when I'd come home after seven years in Vancouver. Beau and I had been strangers then.

Now it felt that way again. For a minute neither of us said anything. We just studied each other. My first sensation was relief. I'd been bracing myself to find a gaunt and hollow-eyed ghost of the kid brother I remembered. But Beau looked okay. He was thin, all right—especially his face. The childhood roundness was gone, leaving it sculpted with hard angles where the softness used to be. He was a little pale for a country kid in May but that just made his eyes seem darker. If Beau was about to die, I thought bitterly, he was going to make one handsome corpse.

The silence between us was getting heavy. What did I do now? Shake his hand? Hug him? I couldn't recall having ever hugged my brother. What did I say? Hi, Beau, sorry to hear you're dyin'?

I could see that Beau felt the tension too. Finally he broke the silence. "Should've known you'd show up in the rain and track up the floor again."

"How could I help it? Never does anything but rain in this godforsaken country."

Beau grinned and opened the door wide. "Yeah? Well, it hardly rained at all last summer so if havin' you show up is what it takes to get the grass to grow I guess it's worth it. Don't just stand there. Come on in."

I took a step inside but he held up a hand like a traffic cop. "Take off the boots."

I laughed. Good ol' Beau. Since there weren't any women around, and Pop tended not to notice things like house-cleaning, Beau had generally got stuck with it. It made him sensitive about a little mud. "Okay, okay." I reached for the bootjack. "So, where were you headed just now?"

He gave me a puzzled look. "What do you mean? I wasn't goin' anywhere." I guess I looked puzzled now, my eyes on the smoke-gray Stetson he was wearing. It was a nice hat and it must have set him back a few bucks, but I still didn't see why he'd want to wear it around the house. He caught the direction of my gaze, and the look that crossed his face just then flashed me back to when he was seven and his dog got run over right in front of him. Then, the pain was gone—or at least disguised by a grin. "Welcome home, Steve," he said, and swept off the hat. He was totally bald.

I stared, mentally cursing myself for being so stupid. Of course—the chemotherapy. People taking chemo always lost their hair. Yeah, *people* did. But not Beau. For some crazy reason the thought of my brother losing his hair—that great wavy, streaky-blond hair he was so proud of and always wore long enough to keep Pop belly-aching about it—hit me harder than the thought that he might be losing his life.

"Aw, Beau, not your hair!" And then all the awkwardness between us was gone. The next thing I knew we had our arms around each other and he was sobbing on my shoulder. And hugging my brother felt so good I wondered why I hadn't done it a long time ago.

Beau didn't cry for long. He broke loose, wiped a sleeve across his face and stared me right in the eye. "It'll grow back," he said with a defiant grin, "and when it does it'll be better than yours. Always was better than yours."

"In your dreams, kid. Only in your dreams."

He gave me a good punch on the shoulder. I returned it gently, in case he was breakable or something. He punched me on the other shoulder, not gently, and I returned that one, not as gently as before. Then, all of a sudden he reached up and messed up my hair so bad I could hardly see out. My own hand was halfway to his head when it froze in midair.

"Gotcha!" He said with a killer grin and we both broke out laughing so hard my bruised ribs nearly killed me.

Right about then Pop came out of the kitchen, wiping his hands on a dish towel. It was nearly nine o'clock but he seemed to be cooking supper. "Well," he said, looking me over. "Look what the cat dragged in out of the rain. You look a little the worse for wear." Then he grinned and wrapped his arms around me in a bear hug, and my ribs got it again. He stepped back and looked me over again and his face turned serious. "I'm real glad you're here, son," he said, his voice sounding sort of choked, and I figured if this kept up all three of us tough Garrett boys were soon going to be sharing a carton of Kleenex.

Fortunately, at that moment Beau took a glance through the kitchen door. "You got something important in that red bowl on the table, Pop?" he asked.

"Yeah. Why?"

"Well, Waylon's up there polishing it off." Pop let out a yell and pitched the wadded-up dishtowel into the kitchen like a fastball. There was a yowl and the sound of claws digging for traction on the slippery tabletop, and then both Waylon and the red bowl hit the floor. Waylon got out of there fast and Pop went off, muttering something about making potatoes and gravy but he sure hoped we liked just potatoes 'cause that's what we were having now.

"Where's Willie?" I asked. Waylon and Willie were two kittens somebody abandoned at Pop's gate two or three years ago. Good old hard-as-nails Pop took them in and now, judging from the glimpse I caught of Waylon, they were about the size of overweight bobcats and still growing.

"Asleep on my bed last I saw. You're soaked. Come and get some dry clothes on. Where's your stuff?"

"Well, uh, actually I'm wearin' it."

Beau groaned and shook his head. "Not again." I guess he hadn't forgotten—or forgiven—the fact that I wore out half of his clothes last time I showed up with nothing but the shirt on my back. He took me upstairs and tossed me a worn pair of jeans and a faded t-shirt. "You can have these. They're gettin' too baggy on me anyhow."

Yeah, I thought, because you've lost a lot of weight since you've been sick. But a warning look told me we weren't about to discuss that subject right now, and I was more than happy to leave it alone.

By the time we got back downstairs, Pop had supper on the table—he'd managed to whip up some more gravy from somewhere—and I ate roast beef and potatoes and gravy like I'd never seen food before. That is, I did until Beau suddenly pushed back his chair, took his plate, and scraped his barely-touched supper into the cats' dishes. "Sorry, Pop. It's good but I guess I'm just not that hungry. Think I'll go lie down for a while."

Pop nodded. "Okay, Beau. No problem," he said, calmly, as Beau walked out of the kitchen and headed for the stairs.

I gave Pop a look. Why was he acting so calm about this? I started to stand up but he laid a hand on my arm. "Leave him be,

Steve. It happens all the time. He eats when he feels like it. If he can't, he can't and he sure don't want to be fussed over."

About then I pretty much lost interest in eating and Pop and I limped silently through the rest of the meal. We didn't even argue about who was going to do the dishes. When they were done Pop put on his jacket. "Come on," he said. "I got somethin' to show you."

I followed him outside. It had quit raining now and the yard smelled like growing grass and wet spruce trees. Pop took me over to the garage and opened the door. Up until that moment I hadn't even thought about it, but there it was in all its Plum Crazy Purple glory. My old Charger. I'd driven it in from Vancouver last time I was here and had to abandon it when Romero cornered me over at the Quarter Circle horse sale. I ran a hand over its glossy flank—fender, I mean. Sometimes I get to treating cars like horses. Especially this one. If it had been a horse, it would have been a thoroughbred. I'd customized it so it could outrun anything on the road, including the cops, which I'd proved to Beau and his girlfriend Raine by accident last time I was here.

My hand came away clean. Not a speck of dust. I gave Pop a questioning look. "You took her out and washed her when you knew I was comin' home?"

Pop shook his head. "Not me. Ever since you took off without it Beau's been washing her every few weeks, keeping air in the tires and driving her around the block just often enough to keep the battery charged."

"No kiddin'? He might as well have been drivin' her all the time. I wouldn't have cared."

"Too risky without insurance and up-to-date license. And gettin' them would've led to too many questions. He just said he wanted it to be in shape for you when you came back."

"What made him think I was ever comin' back?"

Pop shrugged and a slow grin spread across his face. "Beats me. He just said you'd be back when the time was right." The smile disappeared. "And I guess the time is right now."

"Yeah." We started to walk back to the house but then I remembered something. "I'll be back in a minute," I said and headed back to the car, popped the trunk, and looked inside. But it wasn't there. I shrugged and went back to the house.

I paced restlessly around the room for the first time in over a year, really wishing I had a cigarette.

Pop was sitting in his beat-up recliner with his feet up, resting his bad knee. He had a *Western Horseman* open in front of him but I could feel his eyes on me. "This is hittin' you pretty hard, ain't it, Steve?" he said at last.

I swallowed and stared out the window into the darkness. "Yeah," I said, "and it must be hittin' you just as hard."

"I reckon so," he said, "but I'm a lot older and the scar tissue's thicker so the pain don't show so much."

"It's not fair, Pop!" I hadn't meant to say the words. They just came out. "Beau doesn't deserve this."

Pop made a sound that might have been a laugh if it hadn't been so bitter. "Of course it ain't fair. You been spendin' your time in some magic kingdom where life is fair, Steve?"

"Not exactly."

"That's right. Life's not exactly fair to Beau or to you or to me—or to the Queen of England for that matter. Just when you

60

think you've got the world by the tail, the sucker busts loose, knocks you over, and kicks you a couple of times when you're down. And about the only thing you can do is get up, rearrange your teeth, and grab hold again."

I shook my head. "It should have been me, Pop, not Beau. All he ever did was work hard, stay out of trouble, and try to make something of himself. I've been in enough scrapes I should have been dead a dozen times, and here I am, healthy as a horse. So why does the good kid get shafted while the bad one gets off scot-free?" My voice went kind of funny on me and I turned away again before Pop could see the tears. But I heard him ease himself out of his chair. I heard his footsteps, the first couple uneven until the knee limbered up.

Then his hard, callused hand was on my shoulder. "You're not so bad, Steve. You're a little bit wild and crazy sometimes and kind of a maverick like your old man, but you're not so bad."

I think that was the closest Pop had ever come to saying he loved me. It felt kind of strange—and kind of good—but it didn't make me feel any better about Beau.

"It's been a long day," I said. "Think I better get some sleep." I turned away and headed up the stairs. At the top I stopped and looked back. "Pop?" I said. "Thanks." I turned away and kept walking before I made a complete fool of myself.

I was halfway up the stairs when Pop's voice stopped me. "Don't make any plans for tomorrow afternoon. You've got an appointment with the doctor."

I was just about to say "What for?" when my brain clicked into gear. "To find out if my bone marrow matches?"

"Yeah. At least to find out if you're healthy enough to be a donor first of all."

I stood there, letting it sink in. This was really going to happen. I wasn't stuck in the middle of some soap opera. Starting tomorrow I was heading down the magic road that was going to save my brother's life—or not. Then another thought hit me. "You didn't call the doctor tonight," I said.

"'Course not," Pop said gruffly. "You think you can just phone a doctor any old time like a pizza place? I made the appointment yesterday."

"I was still in Montana yesterday. How'd you know I'd be here by tomorrow?"

Pop grinned. "I knew," was all he said.

Chapter 10

BEAU WAS ALREADY IN THE SAGGY old double bed we'd shared when I was here before. He looked like he was asleep so I undressed real quietly. Then I just stood there in the middle of the floor, suddenly feeling kind of awkward.

Then I felt Beau's eyes on me. "Well, you comin' to bed or you just gonna stand there in your underwear all night?"

"Uh… look, Beau, maybe I should just unroll my sleeping bag here on the floor. I don't want to keep you awake or anything." Somehow it didn't seem right to make somebody as sick as he was get along with half a bed.

"Do you *have* a sleeping bag, Steve?"

"Well, no but…"

Beau's eyes smoldered. "Don't worry, I'm not contagious if that's what's on your mind."

"No, that's not what's on my mind," I said, feeling like a total fool. "I'm sorry, okay?" I pushed my hair back out of my eyes and wondered how I could be handling this so bad. "It's just that I don't know what you need or what's gonna make things worse for you and…" My voice trailed off.

Beau breathed a deep sigh. "Steve," he said, his voice tired, "couldn't you just treat me like your stupid kid brother like you always did?"

I grinned. "Okay then, move over stupid, you got over half the bed."

"That's better," Beau said, and before I knew what was happening he'd heaved a pillow and hit me right in the kisser. I heaved it back and we spent some time wrecking the joint. Not as much as we would have before, though. On about the fourth throw Beau caught the pillow, lay back on it, breathing hard, and closed his eyes. I took the hint, climbed into bed, and shut off the light. For a while we just lay there in silence.

At last I asked softly, "Beau? You asleep?"

"Nope. Are you?"

"Hey, that used to be my line."

I saw the flash of his teeth as he smiled in the dark. "Yeah? Well, your stupid kid brother ain't as stupid as he used to be."

"Stupid enough to put a whole lot of time and trouble into a car you couldn't even use," I said.

"Should I take that comment to mean thank you?"

"Yeah, I think you should. The old Plum looks great." I paused and then added a question. "You don't happen to know what happened to the couple of hundred bucks worth of new clothes I had packed in my duffel bag in the car, do you?"

The teeth flashed again. "You were wearin' some of them this afternoon."

"You stole my clothes?"

"Borrowed, Steve. Just borrowed. Didn't I share 'em when you needed 'em?"

"Should I take that as a thank you?" We both laughed but a minute later I couldn't help asking the question that was on my mind. "So, how long have you known?"

A faint beam from the yard light caught his eyes as he turned to look at me. "About having leukemia, you mean?"

"Yeah."

"I don't know exactly. Looking back, I guess I should have known something was wrong six months or more ago. I kept gettin' so tired. But I just kept tellin' myself it was nothin'. Just needed to get more sleep. Guess it was about Christmas when I passed out throwin' bales to the horses at the Quarter Circle. I ended up in the hospital, had about a million tests, and when the results came back," his voice dropped to a whisper, "I knew."

"I guess it's been pretty rough."

There was a pause. "Aw, it hasn't been that bad," he said, but I knew he was lying.

I reached over and squeezed his shoulder. "You and me are gonna beat this thing, Beau."

"I'm still mad at you for coming home, you know," he said, but before I could argue he added, "but I'm real glad you're here." His hand came up and gripped my wrist, hard. We lay like that for a while, feeling each other's strength, feeling the blood flow through each other's bodies. The blood we shared. Garrett blood. It was what made us brothers. And I hoped it was what was going to save my brother's life. Beau's hand finally let go. "Night, Steve," he said, and turned on his side.

"Night, Beau." I didn't expect to get to sleep for a long time. Sleep never did come easy for me.

But it had been a long, hard day and I was starting to drift when Beau's voice, sounding sleepy too, brought me back. "Pop's been looking for Mom."

"Is she lost?" That didn't come out quite the way I meant it. Mom had been lost to Pop—and remarried to a real estate sales-man—for over ten years. As far as I knew they still lived in Calgary. Pop could have found her anytime he wanted.

"Pop phoned the real estate company. Ron's not working there any more. They said he'd moved to Denver."

"No kiddin'?" I'd been through Denver a few months back. It was weird to think that my mother had been living there and I never knew it. I wondered if I'd have recognized her if I met her on the street after ten years. Would she recognize me? Would she want to? She'd pretty much given up on me when she left. She'd taken Beau with her, and he'd lived with her and Ron till he was old enough to fight to come back to Pop. But she and I hadn't seen each other since she left.

"Why'd Pop want to find Mom so bad?" As soon as the words were out I regretted them. Why do you think, stupid? Even if she wasn't much of a mother, Pop probably figured she had a right to know her son might be dying.

But that wasn't what Beau meant. "Because Pop didn't know if he could find you," he said. "You're my full brother so you're the best chance for a transplant match, but parents sometimes match—or half-brothers and sisters."

Yeah, Mom did have a new family, but I'd never seen them so they didn't seem quite real to me. "Mom's got two kids, hasn't she?"

"No, actually she's only got one. She looked after her sister's little boy for nearly a year while her sister and brother-in-law were working in Saudi Arabia but she's really only got Jacey."

"Is that a boy or a girl?"

"A girl. She was a real little terror last time I saw her. Cute, though."

"All of Mom's kids were cute," I said with a yawn.

Beau laughed. "And terrors too, huh, Steve?"

"You were. I wasn't, but then you never knew me when I was little enough to be a terror."

"Thank God," Beau muttered sleepily.

Chapter 11

I WOKE UP WITH THAT UNEASY FEELING that something was wrong but I couldn't remember what. For a second I didn't know where I was. Then I remembered. Pop's place. I was here because Beau was sick. I was back sharing the same old room and the same old lumpy mattress we'd slept on last time I was here. It was just gray dawn outside. Beau would still be sleeping. But he wasn't. When I glanced over at his side of the bed he was half sitting up with his pillow jammed behind him, and his head leaned back against the head of the bed. His eyes were closed but I knew he was awake.

I sat up. "Beau?"

He opened his eyes. "Hi, Steve," he said with a tired grin.

"How come you're not sleepin'?" I checked the clock. "It's not even six o'clock yet."

"Can't."

"You feelin' worse?"

He shook his head. "Not really. It just hurts sometimes."

"Where?"

He shrugged. "All over. My joints. Sometimes my head. Don't worry about it. It's normal."

I swallowed. Yeah, it was normal—if you had a disease that was slowly killing you. Before I could think of anything to say Beau changed the subject. "Raine's comin' over this morning."

He threw the words out as casual as a weather forecast, but they struck me like lightning. Raine, Beau's gray-eyed, strawberry blond girlfriend. The girl I'd half-fallen in love with last time I was here—and almost lost my brother's trust forever by doing it.

Beau yawned and eased over onto his side. "Think I might be able to get back to sleep now. I might not be awake when she gets here and I think Pop's gotta go to town, so you can entertain her for a while, okay?"

I stared hard at my brother and tried to read what was on his mind. Just like that he throws Raine and me together alone. Why? Because he's sure enough of himself—and Raine—to know there's nothing left between her and me? Or because he's not sure at all and wants to put us to the test for once and for all? Or—and the third possibility sent a sliver of ice through my insides—does he think he's not going to be around so Raine and I might as well be together?

Beau's face was in the shadows but I could feel his eyes on me, waiting for an answer. "Sure," I said, real casual. "I'm lookin' forward to seein' her again."

"Good." Beau yawned again, buried his face in the pillow, and gave a deep sigh. Two minutes later, as far as I could tell, he was sound asleep. I lay there staring at the ceiling for half an hour and then gave up and got dressed.

Pop and I had breakfast together. Then he took off to deliver a saddle he'd just finished making for a guy in town. I got stuck with the dishes, but even that was better than just hanging around waiting.

I didn't have to wait for long. It was just past eight when I heard hoofbeats coming down the lane. Somehow that surprised me. Raine was eighteen now and I thought she might have kind of grown out of horses. I was wrong. I stepped out onto the porch just in time to see her come around the bend, riding hell-bent for leather just the way I remembered her from three years ago. But then she'd been riding Fox, her golden-sorrel mare with a mane the same color as Raine's.

This time the horse was a jet-black stallion—Rebel Yell, the black-hearted devil that had spent weeks trying to kill me when I tried to break him to ride. That same horse turned around and saved my life by making the jump and run of a lifetime when Romero was shooting at me. I guessed that day was the beginning of the end of Rebel's outlaw days, but he was still plenty of horse to handle. Some people would say he was no horse for a girl to be riding—but I wouldn't want to be standing too close if Raine heard them say it. Anyway, she was doing just fine as far as I could see.

"Whoa, Reb!" She hollered, and settled back in the saddle as the big horse came to a sliding stop. Not only was she riding that horse, she had put a whole lot of training into him. Now she was looking at me like she was seeing a ghost. "Steve?"

"Hey, Raine," I said.

"I can't believe you're really here. Your dad's been looking for you for weeks and I was so scared he wouldn't find you in time. The transplant has to work. Beau is so sick and he just keeps getting worse..." Her voice broke and she swallowed hard.

"I know," I said. "It's gonna work." I changed the subject. "Rebel looks good. You must have had a few western moments before you got him to this stage."

She laughed. "Oh, he unloaded me a couple of times if I did something that offended his Royal Highness. But he's actually been a pretty good boy." She jumped down and held the reins out to me. "Here, take him for a run. After all the times he dumped you in the dirt it isn't fair that you only got to ride him once."

I grinned, remembering. "Yeah, but that was the time that counted." That was the day of the horse at the Quarter Circle, Raine's parents' ranch, where I'd worked a couple of months training horses. And the day Carlos Romero caught up to me. He had me cornered, a gun in his hand, and I thought it was all over—until my brother hit him with an all-star football tackle that knocked him off balance long enough for me to make a break for it. And, in the second it took for Romero to steady his gun again, I took the biggest gamble of my life—jumped on the black stallion who'd dumped me a few dozen times before, and gave him the spurs. And, for the first time in his life, Rebel hadn't bucked. He cleared a five-foot fence and ran hard enough and fast enough that Romero's bullet went through my arm instead of my heart. I owed that horse.

I also owed my brother, I reminded myself as I reached out to take the reins from his girlfriend and our hands touched. I had to keep reminding myself as she looked up at me and I found myself in danger of drowning in the depths of those gray eyes again.

I kept my attention on the horse. "Easy, Reb," I said softly, rubbing his forehead. "Remember me?" Apparently he did. He chose that moment to give a big nose-blowing snort and cover me with a fine spray of horse snot. We were still buddies.

I gathered up the reins and swung into the saddle. For a second I felt him freeze—go stock still without even so much as a quiver. I'd felt that stillness before. It meant that in about two seconds he was going to explode. This was going to be interesting. "Okay, Reb. Let's get it over with." I gave him a light nudge with my heels. I felt his back muscles relax and he moved off in a lope so smooth I could have carried my coffee and never spilled a drop. Rebel Yell was broke to ride. I was almost disappointed.

I probably rode for nearly an hour. I don't suppose this was what Beau had in mind when he told me to entertain Raine, but it was a lot safer. When I walked Rebel slowly back into the yard, cooling him down, Beau was up. He and Raine were leaning on the corral fence talking. Raine looked up. "Hey, I told you to try him out, not steal him." Then she smiled. "So, what d'you think?"

"Aw, he's not too bad, considering he's been trained by a girl," I said, and Raine threw a horse brush at me and almost put my eye out. We were getting along just fine.

"Hey, Steve," Beau said with a puzzled look on his face. "You know some guy named Leroy? He phoned a while ago and I never did figure out what he was sellin' but it seemed real important to let you know he was callin' from his momma's place in Spokane."

"Right on," I said, and headed for the house. I had a doctor to see in a couple of hours.

Chapter 12

MY APPOINTMENT WITH DR. ADDERSLY was at eleven o'clock. I hadn't left myself much time but Beau let me drive his truck and it had a fair number of horses under the hood. I checked the time as I walked into the waiting room. Ten fifty-nine, the clock said. All right! I thought, impressed. I was a punctual kind of a guy.

I might as well have saved my energy. It was eleven-thirty by the time the nurse came out and called me. She led me down the hallway into a little windowless room and nodded toward a blue cotton thing lying folded up on the table. "Okay, Mr. Garrett, just strip and slip into that gown. The doctor will be in shortly."

I stared at her. "Strip?"

"Yes," she said tiredly, like she was dealing with somebody who was a little slow, "you know, undress." Yeah, actually I knew what strip meant. I just hadn't planned on doing it. When Pop had said I needed to go in for a checkup I thought they might listen to my heart, take a blood sample to make sure I didn't have AIDS or something, and pronounce me healthy and fit for spare parts. But things didn't seem to be working out quite that way. The nurse closed the door and left me alone in there.

I picked up the blue thing—gown, I mean. *Gown?* I'd never worn a gown in my life and couldn't see starting now. I'd never even seen one of these things except on TV. I'd been beat up, cut up, and even shot up once, but I'd managed to stay away from doctors. They were a little too anxious to report any suspicious injuries to the cops.

Now I guessed I was about to get a crash course in the world of medicine. Reluctantly I undressed and put on the gown. It reached somewhere above my knees. I tied up the little strings and took a step. The front gaped open in all the wrong places. That's when it occurred to me that I might have the thing on backward. I took it off and tried again. There, that looked better—at least from the front it did. I was pretty sure it was gaping at the back now but at least I couldn't see it.

I inspected the room. Paper-covered examining table. Locked glass-fronted cabinet full of drugs. Automatically I checked the labels, a holdover from my drugs-for-recreation days, I guess. Then I studied an assortment of nasty-looking instruments laid out in a cart next to the examining table, tried to figure out what they were used for, and decided I didn't really want to know. There was a fancy diploma on the wall, proof that B.J. Addersly wasn't just some unemployed bricklayer who'd wandered in off the street. That was reassuring.

I paced the room, gown flapping, buns cooling in the breeze. I was running out of things to look at and starting to get real nervous. I hadn't been in a windowless room this small since I went to jail and that wasn't an experience I liked to remember.

After what seemed like an hour there was a little knock on the door and in walked this woman. She was wearing cotton pants and a t-shirt and she looked about my age. I figured she must be the summer student they hired to go around collecting charts or something. "Hi," she said. "You must be Steve Garrett. I'm Barbara Jean Addersly, Beau's doctor. For the time being, I guess I'm your doctor, too."

We shook hands and I finally thought of something to say. "Beau never told me you were a woman."

She laughed. "Well then I'm way ahead of you. He did mention you were a man. Why don't you hop up on the table there and we'll get this show on the road."

Why don't I? Let me count the reasons… But I hopped up on the table.

Dr. Addersly *did* check my heart, all right, but most everything else got checked, too. Before she was done with me I was feeling like a used car trying to get the A-Okay Seal of Approval to go out on the lot. After I'd coughed and breathed and done a whole lot of difficult stuff she inspected the thin white scar that arcs along the inside edge of my right ribs. She looked at me with a puzzled frown. "Surgery?" she asked.

I laughed. "Guess you could call it that."

"Well, what would you call it?"

"Switchblade," I said.

"Oh."

Then she noticed the round knots of scar tissue on either side of my right biceps. "Hmm, this must have been a fairly severe trauma."

I shrugged. "Yeah, I guess it was kind of traumatic." If she was half the doctor she seemed to think she was she'd know a bullet hole when she saw one. And if she didn't I wasn't about to help her out. She touched the deep knife scar between the two bullet scars. "And this?"

75

I grinned. "Surgery," I said. That really deepened the frown between her eyebrows. But I was telling the truth. I just hadn't explained that the surgery was done by my friend Jesse Firelight with a jacknife by the light of a kerosene lamp in a cow camp cabin in the middle of a blizzard because I was about to die of blood poisoning from that infected bullet wound.

She checked out a few more points of my anatomy, asked a few more questions, commented on a couple more scars, made some notes, and set down her pen. "Okay, Steve, I think that about does it. I'll be back in a couple of minutes and we'll talk."

I was dressed in one minute flat. She took me into her office and sat down behind her desk, motioning me into the other chair. "Well," I said, "did I pass?"

Dr. Addersly smiled. "You know, Steve," she said thoughtfully, "you aren't exactly what I expected of Beau's older brother who's been 'travelling in the States recently.' The scars on your body read like a road map of Trouble County and your lifestyle I can only imagine. For some reason totally beyond my comprehension, however, you seem to be as healthy as a Missouri mule. I'll send you down to the lab for some blood tests, and if those turn out okay the next step will be some tissue matches with Beau."

She walked me to the door and turned to face me for a minute. "I really hope this works out, Steve. Beau's a great kid. He deserves a better break than he's had so far." She turned away fast but not fast enough to see her professional cool slip and her eyes fill with tears.

"Thanks, Doc," I said. I turned away fast, too—for pretty much the same reason.

Chapter 13

I WAS THE ONLY ONE HOME the afternoon that the woman drove up in her shiny red Jeep. It was hot, the deer flies were practicing their circle-and-dive routine around my head, and I was fixing the fence. In other words, I was not in the greatest mood. Since I'd been here last time, Pop had managed to scrape together enough money for him and the bank to actually buy the acreage he'd been renting, so maintenance was up to him now. Or, as it turned out, up to me. Beau had been in the hospital overnight for more tests and Pop had gone to pick him up. The horses were out of grass in the small pasture and whinnying hopefully about being let into the big one.

The fence around the property was mostly imaginary, and since Pop didn't have any fancy machinery, I was pounding posts into the ground by hand. I had on an old pair of dirty, ripped jeans, no shirt, and my hair—which Pop would've said needed cutting—was in my eyes. I was soaked with sweat, streaked with dirt, and, about the time she got out of the jeep, swearing to myself because I'd just jammed a big sliver under my thumbnail. I glanced up in time to see her start across the yard in her designer jeans and expensive boots and thought sourly, Lady, whatever you're sellin', I ain't buyin'.

I ignored her and went back to studying my thumb. When I couldn't put it off any longer I looked up to see what she wanted. She was a pretty good-looking woman—not all that young, maybe thirty-five or forty, but with a good figure, a nice tan, and streaky blond hair (courtesy of an expensive dye job, I figured).

She was giving me a long appraising look, I thought. It was hard to tell where she was looking behind those sunglasses, but I was getting a real stared-at feeling by the time she finally spoke. "Beau?" she said uncertainly. "No, it can't be," she added, more to herself than to me. " Beau can't be out here pounding posts. But you sure look like him." She brushed the hair back out of her eyes and studied my face again. "Steve?" Her voice was even more uncertain now. "But Steve's somewhere in the States..." Her voice trailed off.

In spite of the heat, something cold settled in the pit of my stomach as it dawned on me who this stranger really was. I set the post hammer down and wiped the sweat off my face. "Don't bet on it," I paused, not sure I could actually say the word, "Mom."

It had been over ten years since she drove away and took Beau with her, leaving me and Pop to try to put our world back together. For a while there I thought it was all a mistake and she'd realize it and come back. I guess at eleven I was still in my "Billy the Kid" stage where you think life is a movie and everything will work out in time for the closing credits. By the time I was twelve I knew that wasn't going to happen, and I ran too.

But I should have known her. Parents don't change as much

in ten years as kids do. Slowly, she reached up and took off the glasses. *Then* I knew her for sure. She had the eyes. The smoky, greenish, brownish, grayish eyes that changed color in different lights. I hadn't seen many people with eyes quite that color. Except for Beau and me, that is. I'd always thought of them as Garrett eyes but now I realized that wasn't exactly true. Pop's eyes were blue. The "Garrett" eyes came from Mom's side.

The silence between us stretched out. I let it grow. Mom didn't seem to know what to say to me and I wasn't sure I had anything to say to her. "It's been a long time, Steve," she managed at last.

"Yeah," I said.

"I should have recognized you right away," she said. "I can see now that you're the same old Steve." She tried a smile but when I didn't return it she let it fade.

"Not exactly the same," I said, a little bitterness creeping into my voice. "I've lived a little since then."

She nodded. "So I hear."

I didn't know what she'd heard. Probably mostly the truth. That I'd been mixed up with one of the biggest drug dealers in Vancouver, spent time in jail, and had spent most of the last three years trying to keep from getting caught by the cops or killed by Carlos Romero. It wasn't the kind of story that made you proud to claim somebody as your kid. But then again, she hadn't been proud enough of me to want me around before all that happened. Maybe if she'd stuck around instead of running off with her real estate salesman I'd have stuck around, too, and grown up just being a normal kid like Beau did.

Funny how I'd thought all that was ancient history and that I didn't care about it anymore. Now, with her standing here, I felt all the hurt and anger coming back again. It was like half of me was still that abandoned eleven-year-old. The other half had been around enough to know how to fight dirty.

"Yeah," I said, giving her a long cold look. "I guess you've lived some, too. Did your real estate man give you everything you were missing being stuck with a burned-out cowboy and a couple of bratty kids? Too bad Beau had to interrupt your life in the fast lane by getting sick. If that hadn't happened you could have just kept on pretending this part of your life never existed."

She looked like I'd just slapped her. For a second there I thought she might start to cry, but then she took a deep breath and her eyes flashed. She took a step forward. It crossed my mind that she really *was* going to slap me and I didn't know what I was going to do about it. But instead of hitting me she reached out and grabbed the hand I'd been gnawing on, trying to get the sliver out with my teeth. "Stop that. You'll give yourself blood poisoning."

Before I could figure out what to say the passenger door on the jeep flew open and this little tornado with blond braids and blue jeans came flying across the yard. "Mom! They've got *horses*!" she yelled, pointing over my shoulder to where Spook and Paintbrush had just stepped out of their shed. She focussed on me next. "Are they tame? What are their names? Is that one a paint or a pinto? Are they broke to ride?" She ran out of breath and her mother put a restraining hand on her shoulder.

"WHOA, Jacey," Mom said. Apparently treating her like a horse worked because Jacey stopped asking questions long enough for Mom to say something. "Jacey, run and get the first-aid kit out of the Jeep,"

"But—" said Jacey.

"Go," said Mom.

Jacey went and when she came back Mom silently and efficiently took out the tweezers, pulled out the sliver, and poured some antiseptic over my thumb. "Jacey," she said, but her eyes were on me and there was a question in them. Was I going to agree to a truce for Jacey's sake? "This is your brother, Steve."

I returned Mom's look. Jacey was about ten or eleven, an untamed little outlaw with the kind of wild innocence that was only a distant memory for me. I wasn't about to do anything to mess up her world. I didn't even remind Mom that, technically, it should have been half-brother.

I held out my hand. "Hey," I said. "It's pretty cool to get a brand-new sister who's already past the diapers and howling stage. Nice to meet you, Jace."

"Yeah, you too, Steve," Jacey said, kind of absent-mindedly, but she shook my hand with a grip that would have made a wrestler flinch. "*Now* can I ride the horses?"

Mom started to say something, but right then Pop's truck turned into the driveway. "Sure, Jace. Ol' Spook'll be glad to give you a ride." I looked at Mom. "Go ahead," I said, "I'll take care of her." I wasn't just being nice. Meeting Mom one-on-one had been bad enough. I was grabbing a real good excuse to stay out of the middle of the family reunion that was about to take place up at the house.

Jacey scowled at me. "I don't need looking after. I just want to ride the horse."

Yeah, Jace, I thought, I know how you feel. I grabbed two halters. We'd both go for a ride.

Jacey and I rode down along the river. She was right. She

didn't need looking after. She rode that big gray horse like she'd been born on his back. Not that Spook gave her any trouble. He had about the best disposition of any horse I'd ever known. That was one reason I'd ended up buying him—sort of—from the abusive idiot that owned him.

Paintbrush was another story. When Pop had mentioned getting the registered paint mare in trade for making a saddle I'd thought he'd come out way ahead. Now, I wasn't so sure. As soon as I hit the saddle, that little mare started in crow-hopping and almost had me unglued before I could pull her head up and settle her down. Jacey enjoyed that whole performance a lot, but I think she was a little jealous that her horse didn't provide a little more excitement.

"I guess Spook never bucks, huh?" she asked, a little disappointment in her voice.

"Naw, Spook's a good ol' boy. He used to be a ropin' horse."

"Really? That would be very cool. Could you teach me to rope, Steve?"

I shook my head. "Truth is, Jace, I never learned to rope. Bet Pop would teach you, though. He used to be pretty good."

Jacey cocked her head and gave me a thoughtful look. "Is that what you call him all the time? Pop?"

"Yup, long as I can remember."

"And he doesn't mind?"

"Never said he did. Should he?"

"My dad would mind. He would think Pop sounded rude."

"Yeah, I bet he would." And if he ever actually met Pop, he'd think Pop *acted* rude too, I added silently.

"You know what, Steve?"

"No, what?"

"Mom said she read somewhere that there were still some wild horses around here somewhere. Is that true?"

"Well, I don't know, Jace. I haven't been around here much lately, but I remember Beau sayin' once that he saw some out west of Sundre somewhere. That's not too far from here."

"We could go look for them someday and maybe I could tame one and bring it back here and you could help me train it and it wouldn't be really mean but it might buck a little like Paintbrush did but I think I could stay on and even if it threw me I'd get back on and—"

"Jacey, WHOA!"

She paused and took a breath. "What?"

"Rein in, kid, you're havin' a runaway."

Automatically, she started to tighten her reins and then she loosened them again and glared at me. "What's that supposed to mean? Spook's not even out of a walk."

"I wasn't talkin' about the horse."

Jacey sighed. "You know Steve, you're startin' to sound just like a grownup," she said tiredly. It took me a while to think that over. I didn't think anybody had ever accused me of that particular crime before and I wasn't sure if I should feel complimented or insulted.

Before I could decide, Jacey spoke up again. "Okay, okay, I know I talk too much. Mom's always tellin' me that. But I *really, really* do want to see some wild horses. Will you take me to look for them when you get a chance? Please, Steve?"

It was my turn to sigh. "Sure, Jace," I said. "If I get a chance." I thought that was a safe enough promise. I didn't expect to get a chance. Jacey was talking like we'd landed here to be one big fairy tale family and live happily ever after. I didn't figure she'd be here long enough for any wild horse chases, and I knew for a fact that if Beau got his bone marrow and got cured I'd be out of here. And a cold chill went through me just thinking it—if he *didn't* get cured I'd be just as gone.

Chapter 14

IT TURNED OUT THAT Jacey would be around longer than I had expected. She was going to get tested for a bone marrow match, too, in case mine didn't work out for some reason. I couldn't see how a half-sibling was going to stand a better chance than a full one, but Mom was determined to check it out. I think Mom had also made up her mind to stick around and spend some long overdue time with Beau—while she still had the chance. Having her around seemed to mean a lot to him so I figured I'd have to live with it—as long as she stayed away from me.

That worked out okay because when Raine's mom found out Beau's mom and sister were going to be around for a while, she invited them to stay over at the Quarter Circle. She's got a big house and a bigger heart, and ever since Beau started working there—even before he started going out with her daughter—she's treated him like family. Come to think of it, she treated me the same way when I worked there for a couple of months, too. I guess she figured she might as well have a few more Garretts in the family.

Before they could do the transplant Beau had to go into the hospital for another blast of chemo so everything was on hold for a while. Between visits to the hospital, Mom and Jacey spent a lot of time at Pop's place. Watching Mom and Pop together was kind of interesting. Considering that they'd once been close enough to have two kids together it was pretty strange to see how they treated each other like polite strangers now.

One evening Mom had actually cooked supper, which was so good that even I had to act like a polite stranger. Afterward I went out and caught Spook and was out behind the shed trimming his hoofs when Mom and Pop came out and sat down on the porch. I could hear them exchanging a few words now and then, but mostly they were just drinking coffee and watching the sun ease down over the horizon. Then, casual as if he was commenting on the weather, Pop asked, "So, how's your real estate man doing? Still making piles of money and keeping you in the lifestyle of the rich and famous?"

I looked around the corner of the shed in time to see Mom give Pop a look I couldn't quite read. I thought she was going to get mad at him but all she said was "Yes, Ron's still doing fine, as far as I know."

Pop looked at her. "What d'you mean, 'as far as you know'?"

Mom sighed. "I wasn't going to tell you this but I guess you might as well know. Ron and I have been separated for a couple of years. It never was working out, but I hung in there for as long as I could to prove to myself that I hadn't made a mistake in marrying him." Silence hung in the air for a long minute and then Mom added, "But it was a mistake. You going to say 'I told you so,' now, Tom?"

Pop slowly shook his head. "Nope," was all he said. Then he grinned and nodded to Jacey, who was halfway up a poplar tree trying to catch Willie. The whole knee was out of her jeans and she had dirt on her face and twigs caught in her hair. "Bet poor old Ron never knew what to do with that undomesticated little outlaw. She acts just like the Garrett kids did at her age."

Mom didn't answer for a real long time but I could see her staring at Pop like he'd just said something unbelievable. Then, her voice so low I barely caught the words, she said, "Jacey *is* a Garrett, Tom."

I froze, trying to take that in, and I saw Pop do the same. "What?" he whispered.

Mom took a deep breath. "You weren't ever supposed to know. But now, with this business with Beau... She's his full sister, Tom. I was pregnant when I left you to marry Ron. I didn't know till after I'd burned too many bridges to look back."

Pop was quiet for a long time. When he finally spoke his voice was soft, but I could hear the hurt in it. "I've got a daughter and you weren't ever going to tell me about her?"

Mom shook her head. "I'm sorry, Tom. I was so mixed up. I'd hurt just about everybody who cared about me. I didn't see any point in coming around to hurt you some more...." Her voice trailed off and the silence grew. She tried again. "I've thought back about our time together more than you'd ever believe, trying to figure out where it all went wrong. We were way too young when we got married..."

Pop gave her a sideways look. "As I recall, Katie, we didn't have a whole lot of choice at the time."

It took a couple of seconds for that comment to sink in. When it did I wondered how anybody could grow up as street-wise as me and still be so ignorant about something that should have been so obvious. But now nobody had to draw me a picture. No wonder Mom and I never got along. I'd started messing up her life even before I was born.

I felt a little guilty listening in on this conversation but it wasn't exactly my fault I was eavesdropping. I'd already been here when the conversation started and I didn't think it would be useful to jump up and yell, "Howdy!" right about now. So I just kept listening and filing off the rough edges of Spook's hoof. Pop said something then that I didn't hear because right then Jacey hollered, "Come on down, Willie! You know I can climb as far as you can!" But I heard Mom's answer, which was actually a question.

"What's going to happen to him, Tom?"

Pop didn't answer for a minute. Then, so low, that I barely caught the words, he said, "What I'm really scared is gonna happen is that if he doesn't manage to straighten out his life, is he'll wind up dead before he hits twenty-five."

At first I thought he was talking about Beau. Wasn't that what was on everybody's mind, Beau winding up dead? But then the rest of that sentence registered. Straighten out his life? If Beau's life was any straighter he wouldn't be able to walk around corners. That was me they were talking about. I gave the hoof file an extra hard pull, slipped and filed a piece of skin off my knuckle. I swallowed a loud, "Ouch!" and, mercifully, Mom and Pop got up and walked into the house.

I went for a long walk.

Chapter 15

THE DOCTORS CHECKED both my blood and Jacey's to see how close something called our HLA antigens matched Beau's. I didn't follow all the technical details but both of us turned out to be pretty much equally acceptable donors. The question of which one to choose would be settled at a meeting on Monday but Jacey and I had our own meeting on a walk through the hayfield on Saturday.

"So," Jacey said thoughtfully, "all that HLA stuff the doctor was talking about means my bone marrow would be just as good for Beau as yours, right?"

"Yeah, that's what it means."

"So somebody has to decide who gets to give it to him, huh?"

"Right again, Jace."

"I wouldn't be scared, you know."

I had to smile. As far as I could see there was nothing on earth that scared Jacey. "I know you wouldn't."

"Would you, Steve?"

"Sure, I guess I would be—a little. I've never been knocked out and operated on before."

"I have. They took my appendix out when I was seven. It

wasn't so bad. I didn't even throw up."

"Were you supposed to throw up?" All this surgery stuff was new to me. I felt a little ignorant getting my medical information from a ten-year-old.

"Some people throw up from the anesthetic. But I didn't. I never throw up. So I should probably be the one they operate on." She gave me a hard look "This isn't gonna be one of those things they try to stop me from doin' because I'm a girl, is it?"

I had a feeling Jacey had already fought a few battles on that subject and would fight—and probably win—a whole lot more before she was finished. "Naw, I don't think bein' a girl counts with this kind of stuff."

"Good. So, I get to do it?"

"I didn't say that. The doctors probably get to make the final decision, but we could draw straws to see who volunteers in case we get to decide."

She cocked her head sideways and thought for a few seconds. "Okay."

I picked some long stems of timothy hay and broke one off short. I laid two in the palm of my hand and showed them to her. "Short straw gets to do it?"

"Okay," she said again.

"Watch out!" I yelled. "Snake!" I pointed at a narrow dark shape lying motionless among the tall hay stems. She glanced down and I slid a spare long-stemmed piece out of my sleeve and edged the short one up to replace it.

Jacey gave me a pained look. "Steve, are you losin' it or what? There aren't any snakes in this part of Alberta. That's just an old stick."

I shrugged. "Sorry, Jace. I had a bad experience with a snake back in Montana and I've been kinda nervous ever since."

Jacey studied me with new interest. "Did he bite you?"

"Naw, he just crawled over me."

"That's nothin'," she said, sounding a little disappointed. "Come on, let's draw."

I held out my hand, covering the ends of the stems. Jacey drew a long stem and I opened my hand and gave my sleeve an inconspicuous shake. The other two stems disappeared into the tall standing hay.

"Too bad, Jace. You lose."

She stared at me for a few long seconds, a puzzled frown on her face. "If I looked hard enough I probably could find those stems you just dropped," she said.

"Yeah, but you don't want to do that."

"You cheated, didn't you Steve?" Those Garrett eyes of hers were looking right into my soul—a place I don't particularly enjoy having closely inspected.

I sighed. "Yeah, Jace, I guess I did."

"Why?"

"Cause Beau probably saved my life once and I'd really like to do the same for him."

Jacey was quiet for a minute. Then she nodded. "Okay, Steve, if it means that much to you. But next time just tell me. Don't treat me like a dumb little kid."

You got it, Jace, I thought. If anybody's dumb around here it sure isn't the little kid.

Chapter 16

IN THE END, the doctors decided I would be the best donor anyway. An adult would be able to handle the procedure better. The "procedure" turned out to be a lot different than I had expected. They weren't going to knock me out, jab a big needle into my hipbone, and suck out a few dozen syringes full of marrow after all. Now, I found out they had a new method where they just sat you down in a big recliner, made a hole in your jugular—or some equally scary vein—pumped all your blood out, and ran it through a machine that collected the stem cells. Oh, yeah, they keep pumping the blood back into you when they've got the stem cells out, so you never really run short of it. It didn't exactly hurt but it wasn't real comfortable either, and it took a couple of sessions of about five hours each. When they selected the "adult" for this job they didn't consider the fact that I'd probably never sat still for five hours at a time in my entire life. To "relieve the boredom" there was a TV. As far as I was concerned, five hours of soap operas was definitely the most painful part of the procedure.

The day before they were going to do the transplant I went to see Beau. To kill all the cancer cells they'd been blasting him with enough chemicals to knock off an elephant—and killed off a lot of good cells as well—so he could get a clean start with my stem cells. They'd destroyed most of his immunity in the process so that any old everyday germ could knock *him* off. To avoid that, anybody who visited had to mask up like a doctor about to perform open-heart surgery. It didn't make for relaxed visiting, but that's the way it was.

Mask on my face, I walked in. "Hey, Beau," I said. It came out kind of muffled, but Beau opened his eyes and gave me a long look.

He said something but his voice was so low I almost didn't catch it. He gestured toward the mask. Then I got it. "Billy the Kid," he'd said, and now he added, "You look like you're about ready to rob a train."

"Nope," I said. "This time I'm not stealin' from the rich, I'm givin' to the poor."

Beau propped himself up on an elbow. "What are you plannin' to give to who?" Then he caught on. "You mean the stem cells?"

"Yup, the vampires in the doctor suits drained me for two whole afternoons. You better take care of those little cells when you get 'em. They're used to livin' in high-class accommodation."

Beau curled his lip scornfully. "Yeah, right. All that clean livin' you're so famous for. My body'll likely reject them for its own protection."

"It better not," I said, dead serious now. Rejection was all too good a possibility.

Beau turned serious, too. "It won't," he said, but I could see he was trying to convince himself as much as me. He laid back and closed his eyes for a minute. Then he looked up at me again. "So, I guess I'm about to become your blood brother as well as your regular brother now."

"Guess so," I said with a grin. "Scary, huh?"

He gave me a long look. "Definitely scary," he said, and then added, "And, as Jacey would say, very cool." He reached out a hand. I probably wasn't supposed to touch him but I did. Our hands met in a steel grip that held till we heard the nurse coming.

Beau let go. "Get outta here before you get me into trouble— as usual," he whispered.

I waved goodbye and didn't look back as I walked away.

I'd like to be able to say that one shot of my excellent stem cells and Beau was up playing basketball. Unfortunately it didn't happen that way. If anything, he just kept getting sicker. I went in to see him a couple of times in those first two weeks, but the doctors were real strict about how many could go in and for how long. With Raine and Pop and Mom sitting there waiting, you practically had to take a number to get a chance to go in. Mom and I pretty much avoided each other whenever we could. From what I could see she seemed genuinely concerned about Beau, but I still didn't think it made up for all the time she'd spent for- getting all about even having her first two kids.

I was sitting with Beau one afternoon. He was so tired he could hardly keep awake but he seemed to want me there, and every once in a while he'd open his eyes and say something. Sometimes it didn't even make much sense. Out of the blue one day he just looked up at me and said, "You don't like her much, do you?"

"Who?" I said, totally confused. Was he checking to make sure I really wasn't going to make a play for Raine?

"Mom," he said. "You make real sure you're never around when she is. You still haven't forgiven her, have you?"

I didn't answer that question. Instead I said, "Look, Beau, I'm glad she's here for you, and you and her are gettin' along good. You and her have history. You lived with her for a lot of years even if, in the end, you decided you'd rather live with Pop. My history with her ended the day she took you and drove away without ever lookin' back."

Beau shifted uncomfortably and I could see he was hurting. I wished he'd just drop this subject and try to go back to sleep. But he wasn't about to. He shifted again so he could look up at me better and then he said, real quiet, "She wanted to take you, you know."

"Yeah, sure she did," I said, not quite able to keep the bitterness out of my voice. "If she'd wanted to, she would have. You were the good kid. I was the one who was always makin' waves. She didn't need that much trouble in her life, so she left me for Pop to try to deal with."

"I thought that for a long time, too," Beau said. "Up until last year, when I found the letter."

"What letter?"

"The one Mom wrote to Pop a few weeks after she took me and left. When my class went on the biology field trip to the coast last year I needed to borrow Pop's old duffel bag. He said it was in his closet and to help myself. When I was diggin' around in there I knocked this box of dusty old stuff off the shelf. There were some of our baby pictures and the letter. Go look in my jeans there in the closet. I've been hangin' onto it, waitin' for the right time to show it to you."

I wasn't so sure that this was the right time, or if I even wanted to see this letter, but I knew Beau wasn't about to let me out of there until I read it. It was folded up and you could see from the wear on the folds that it had been around a while and read more than a few times.

I recognized Mom's swirly writing.

Dear Tom,

I'm sure hearing from me right now isn't exactly going to make your day, but please believe me when I say that I hope things are going okay for you. Beau and I are fine but I'm beginning to realize that I made a terrible mistake leaving Steve with you. He's so vulnerable right now that I'm afraid he's going to get into real trouble soon. I don't have to tell you how much trouble he's already been in at school. I know you think the world of him and will do your best, but the more I think about it the more I feel he needs to be with his mom and brother. And, to tell you the truth, in spite of everything, I miss him terribly. I know you've got no reason to do anything to make my life better at this point, but would you please consider letting him come to live with us—even for a year or two? Just till he gets a little older and gets used to the idea that our old life on the ranch is over, for all of us.

I'm sorry everything had to get so messed up between us, Tom. Please think about what I'm asking, for Steve's sake. I couldn't stand to see him ruin his life somehow.

Kate

I finished reading and looked up to meet Beau's eyes. "So, I guess his answer was no. Pop never mentioned anything about this to me."

"Check the date on the letter."

I did and then I understood. Beau put it into words for me. "When she wrote that letter you had already run away. She never got a second chance with you." He paused and then added, "Mom made a lot of mistakes. She knows that now. But not lovin' you wasn't one of them. She told me how bad she feels that you think she didn't want you around."

Somehow hearing all that just made me angrier. "Jeez, Beau, is that what you and Mom do during all the time she spends with you—analyze me? Maybe you should call up one of those TV shrinks and we could all go on the network and share little Steve's childhood hang-ups with a few million people." I stood up, took a deep breath, and calmed down. "Sorry, Beau. I know you're just tryin' to make everybody into one big happy family again. But it won't work. If Mom's got somethin' to say to me, maybe she should try sayin' it herself."

"Maybe she would if you ever tried sticking around to listen to her."

I looked at my watch. "I gotta go, Beau. It's past visiting hours."

"Chicken," Beau said as I walked away.

Chapter 17

ALMOST TWO WEEKS HAD PASSED now since they'd done the transplant and things weren't looking too great. I hadn't been in to see Beau since we'd had that last argument, but Pop and Mom were in there every day. They were pretty worried about how sick and weak Beau seemed to be. The doctors weren't making any promises about which way things were going. Nobody said much about it in front of Jacey, but she didn't need anybody to draw her a picture. She knew how close to the edge Beau was and it was hitting her as hard as the rest of us.

Dad was back at the hospital with him again today and Mom had to go to the dentist, so Jacey and I were hanging out at home. I was out by the barn fixing a broken bridle rein and Jacey wasn't doing much of anything. For once she wasn't even talking my ear off.

"Is he gonna get better, Steve?" Jacey asked at last, looking at me with those soul-searching eyes.

I took a deep breath, considered a lie, and then decided Jacey deserved better. "I don't know, Jace. He's in pretty bad shape right now. But Beau's a fighter. If anybody can get over this he can."

She thought that over. "I've been sayin' a lot of prayers for him," she said. "Now I guess all we can do is have faith." She paced restlessly over to the fence and stood leaning on a rail, making patterns in the dust with her scuffed riding boot. "But this hanging around not being able to do anything to help is really getting on my nerves."

Yup, I thought, this kid really is my sister. I felt the same way but it didn't seem fair that a little kid like Jace should have to be worrying like this. Suddenly I remembered something that might just turn her day around. "Hey," I said. "You know what I heard at the feed store this morning?"

"What?" Jacey asked, still looking at the ground and scuffing dust.

"A guy who'd just come back from camping up by the Ram River Falls said he saw a whole herd of wildies up there yesterday."

Jacey's foot froze in mid-scuff. If she'd been a horse she would have pricked up her ears and snorted. She just about did it anyway. "No kiddin'? Real wild horses?"

"That's what he said. Half a dozen mares and colts and a palomino stallion."

"Where's the Ram River Falls? How do you get there? Will you take me, please, pretty please Steve—my handsome, intelligent, wonderful brother? How soon can we go?"

That all came out in one breath, and when she was about to turn purple from lack of air she stopped long enough for me to give her the short answers. "Northwest of Sundre. A couple of hours. Yes, I will. And, yes, I am. In ten minutes."

She digested that for a couple of seconds then let out a whoop so loud it scared Waylon off the hay bale where he'd been sleeping and halfway up a tree before he looked back to see what hit him.

I just shook my head. If parenthood was anything like big-brotherhood I was not planning a family anytime soon. "Take it easy, Jace. We need some lunch, some gas, and," I glanced down at my holey jeans, which were just barely clinging to the border of decency, "I need to change my clothes. You're in charge of lunch. Ham sandwiches and coffee would be good. I'll take care of the gas and my clothes."

She gave me a dirty look over her shoulder as she trudged off toward the kitchen. "Wouldn't you know it," she muttered. "The woman always gets stuck with the cooking."

Laughing, I headed upstairs. I'd just pulled on a clean t-shirt and had one leg into my clean jeans when the phone rang. I heard Jacey answer it but I couldn't hear what she was saying until she hollered, "Steve! It's for you." That spooked me a little. I didn't exactly have a wide circle of friends around here. If Pop was calling it could be bad news. If anyone else was calling, them knowing I was here could also be bad news. I yanked my jeans the rest of the way on, and thundered down the stairs. "Hello?"

"Mr. or Mrs. Garrett?" A voice with an accent that made it sound like Mr. or Mrs. Carrot asked. Weird. *Mrs.* Garrett hadn't lived here for a long time—*never* lived here, in fact. What was this all about?

"Yeah, this is Mr. Garrett." Well, it *was* the truth.

"Mr. Carrot, we have an exceptional offer for you today. If we could have just a half hour of your time to come by and show you our revolutionary new Whistleclean carpet cleaner, shop vac, and—"

"Sorry," I interrupted. "You've got the wrong Mr. Carrot." I hung up and glanced over my shoulder at the sound of giggling. Jacey. The little rat had set me up.

"Okay, hotshot, you win that one, but you better watch your back. I'll get even. Now get back to your cookin', woman. I'm goin' to gas up the truck."

But I didn't gas up the truck because when I went into the garage to get the key to the bulk gas tank I saw the Charger. The tires were up; the tank was full. It was the best looked-after car in Alberta, all dressed up with nowhere to go. Well, why not? We were going to be completely on back roads. The chances of getting checked for up-to-date insurance and registration were practically zero. And I had been seriously missing Ol' Plum Crazy Purple. I started her up and backed out of the garage just as Jacey came out of the house with a brown bag and thermos. For once she was speechless as she piled in beside me. "Co-o-ol," she managed at last, and we headed for the hills.

But Jacey wasn't stuck for words for long. She told me all about her school in Denver and how she wasn't sure she wanted to move back to Calgary since all the Alberta kids weren't going to get out for summer holidays for another month and what a lame deal that was. Actually, she'd managed to get out even earlier than normal for the States since Mom had told the school they had to come here right away for an emergency. Then Jacey moved on to the subject of horses, which included a detailed description of every horse she'd ever met and some she'd seen in magazines. I'd pretty much tuned her out and took a minute to return to full consciousness when she asked me a question for the second time. "So what horse was it you bought from that guy, Steve?"

"What guy?"

Jacey sighed impatiently. "The guy who sold you the horse when you were here before."

Now it was my turn to sigh. "Jace, I have no idea who you're talkin' about. I never bought any horses while I was here. I just helped train some to be sold. Who told you I bought a horse?"

"I don't know who it was. Some guy who was talkin' to Mom at the door one day. You and your dad were in town or somewh— Look out!"

Right then a big old granddaddy bull moose came lumbering out of the spruce woods and onto the road without stopping to look both ways. Last time something like that happened, it had been a mulie buck that ran out in front of me when I'd been driving my friend Jesse Firelight's ancient truck, and I ended up upside down in the ditch. But when I hit the brakes on the Charger, she fishtailed and laid some nice rubber but she held the road. When I got her stopped we were sitting sideways across the road watching the moose make a clean getaway as he splashed knee-high through a swamp.

"Co-o-l!" said Jace.

I took a deep breath, untensed my muscles, and got the show back on the road. "Yeah," I said. "A lot cooler than if I'd hit him."

"Moose are really dangerous if you get them upset," Jacey informed me. "They can kill you if they want to. But this friend of mine told me that once her dad was out in the woods and he found a baby moose caught in a fence and he went and helped it get loose and its mother just stood there and watched and never even tried to kill him because she knew he was helping..."

The next several miles were entirely devoted to moose. We were out on the Forestry Trunk Road now, and since it was a weekday and school wasn't out yet, there weren't many tourists. Just a whole lot of wild empty country. Gradually the road climbed and the bends got sharper as the hills got bigger. Jacey finally ran out of moose stories and we drove in peaceful silence for a while, just watching the country slide by.

Chapter 18

JUST WHEN IT WAS beginning to feel like this road would keep going nowhere forever, I spotted a sign for a viewpoint turnout ahead. "How far are we from Ram Falls?" Jacey asked.

"I'm not sure. From the time we've been drivin', it can't be much farther."

"Pull off here. I brought a pair of binoculars. Maybe we can see the wildies grazing down in the valley there somewhere."

I clicked on a signal light to let the truck that had been following a ways behind us know I was hanging a left. "Okay, Jace, we'll give it a try. But don't count on seein' them. It's a big country out here."

"We'll see them," she said. There was no point arguing with her. I stopped the car and we got out. Jacey took the binoculars and started scanning the huge expanse of valley laid out below us. Most of it was heavy spruce woods, but here and there it opened out into little patches of green meadow. She was quiet for longer than I would have believed possible as she took in every inch of the scene below. I poured myself a cup of coffee, took a sip, and felt the roots of my hair tingle. *That* was coffee—with very little water added. I was working up the nerve for another sip when I heard Jacey give a gasp. "They're real, Steve! I see them—a whole herd. And the palomino is the most beautiful thing I've ever seen."

I squinted in the direction she was pointing but every one of those little meadows had a few dark spots scattered across it. Any one of them could have been a horse—or a tree, or a water buffalo—for all I could see. "Where, Jace?"

"Right below that rocky ledge," she said, pointing again. She handed me the glasses. "Here, try these."

I focussed on the spot where she had been looking and did a slow sideways sweep with the glasses. Suddenly a sorrel mare with a buckskin colt jumped out at me. I kept moving the glasses and more horses came into sight. Paints and blacks and bays—and one deep gold palomino with a white mane and tail that almost dragged the ground. He was standing alone, head up, testing the wind and guarding his herd.

I heard gravel crunch behind us, and the thought vaguely registered that the truck had turned off, too. The driver was probably curious about what we were looking at. As I adjusted the binoculars I noticed Jacey turning to look over her shoulder.

"Hey, I know who that is. That's the guy who sold you the horse."

"What horse?" I asked, my mind and my eyes still focussed on the scene in the binoculars. That palomino stallion was like something out of a movie—almost too good to be true.

"The gray horse, he said. Did he mean Spook or...?" Suddenly, it registered. I *had* bought—well, sort of bought, sort of stole—a horse when I was here before. Yeah, it *was* Spook and I'd paid an overgrown gorilla by the name of Russ Donovan

$647.00 and taken Spook after he and I had a little physical dis-
cussion about the way he was abusing the horse. I'd made an
enemy for life and he'd teamed up with my friend Romero to try
to take me out a couple of times before.

I spun around to see Russ Donavan barreling out of his truck
and coming toward us at a run. A dozen thoughts flashed across
my mind in that second. He didn't have a gun—if he had one it
would have been in his hand and pointed at me. But he did have
something in his hand. A tire iron. Okay. If he wanted to play
that way. My hand went for the switchblade in my pocket.
Except that, for the first time in more years than I wanted to
remember, the knife *wasn't* in my pocket. I'd left it in my old
jeans when Jacey called me to the phone. All right, I still had a
chance. I'd faced worse odds than this, but never with my kid
sister caught right in the middle. I played the only card I had
left. "Jacey! Run!" I screamed at her and charged in low to
knock Donovan off his feet. But this time I'd hesitated a split
second too long. As I hit Donovan's knees, the tire iron
slammed into my head with a flash of blinding pain.

Chapter 19

"STEVE? YOU OKAY, STEVE?" Jacey's insistent voice cut through the cobwebs in my head. I tried to sit up without much luck. My hands were tied behind me and my ankles were bound together. Jacey was on the floor beside me, tied hand and foot, too. We were in some kind of a shed—probably some place they used to store maintenance stuff for roads and campgrounds. It was almost dark in here, but in the little bit of gray light that filtered in from a tiny window up near the roof I could see some bags of sand and a pile of split wood.

"Yeah," I muttered, trying to ignore the ache in my head. "I'm okay. He didn't hurt you, did he?"

"Uh-uh. Well, except he grabbed my arm pretty hard after I kicked him." I couldn't help but grin. If only Jacey weighed more than an overgrown rabbit the two of us could have out-fought an army.

"Where are we, Jace?"

She shrugged. "I don't know exactly, but not far from where we were. He pushed me down on the floor of his truck and dumped you in on the seat and then drove downhill for a few minutes. I think this is a campground or something, but I saw a sign that said Group Use Only—By Reservation, so I don't think he was too worried about somebody coming along. He dragged us into this shed, tied us up, and disappeared. After a little while I heard him bringing your Charger down here. You can't miss the sound of that big ol' motor."

She paused for a minute and then added in a smaller voice. "What's gonna happen to us, Steve?" I was glad she didn't wait for an answer before she went on, "We've gotta get away before that guy comes back with some Shakespeare guy. Romeo, I think he said."

In spite of everything, I couldn't help laughing. "I think you mean Romero. How do you know about him?"

"The guy called him on his cell phone. Romeo—Romero—was in Calgary and the big bozo was trying to give him directions to where we were, but his cell kept cutting out so he finally yelled that he'd meet him at Mountain Aire Lodge, and then he took off."

I took a deep breath to make sure my voice came out a lot calmer than I felt right then. "No kiddin', Jace. Any ideas about how we're gonna go about gettin' outta here?"

"Well, we could start by using my knife to cut these ropes."

I came to instant full attention. "Your what?"

"My jackknife, of course," Jacey said patiently, like she was dealing with a real slow learner. "It's in my jeans pocket."

I stared at her in amazement. I had a hazy recollection of Donovan's hands roughly going through my pockets after he slugged me with the tire iron. Yeah, right. Big, dangerous me, whose pockets contained seventy-six cents and a used Kleenex, they search. Meanwhile my little sister, the Girl Scout, has still got her knife.

"Can you reach it?"

She didn't answer. Instead, she stretched out full length and began to squirm. She reminded me of Snake, my too-close acquaintance from the Butte country. Next thing I knew she'd managed to hook a finger in a belt loop and was turning the waistband of her jeans around her skinny middle. About the time I thought she was going to turn blue from twisting herself up so tight, she let out a triumphant, "Yes!" I shifted over so I could see behind her. There was the knife in her still-tied hand.

"Nice goin', Jace!"

"Yeah, but now I've got to get it open." For about five minutes the only sound was her panting and puffing as she tried to line up her hands so she could pull the blade out. Twice she dropped the knife. When it happened a third time she said something you don't really expect to hear from your baby sister. Finally she gave up. "It's no use, Steve. I can't get it. You gotta help me. Here, you hold the knife." She snaked around until we were back to back. I felt the knife push up against my hand and I grabbed it. "Okay," Jacey said. "Hold it real still so I can get the blade out."

I held it but she wasn't having much luck. I could hear her muttering about how, if we ever got out of this mess she was never going to chew her fingernails again. I was about to tell her to hold the knife and let me try to open it when she did a lot of scrambling around back there. The next thing I knew there was a cold little nose against my hand. It felt like Willie looking for a Kitty Crumble. "Got it!" Jacey yelled, and I wiggled a finger to stroke the cold, sharp steel of the blade.

"Hey," I said over my shoulder. "How'd you do that?"

"Used my teeth," she said. "Here, give it back to me and I'll cut you loose." She took the knife and began to saw. I know it's not easy to cut a rope you can't see with your hands tied behind you, but even at that I'd have to say Jacey wasn't real skillful at this part. She was digging away with that knife like she was cultivating the garden. I winced as it slipped for about the fifth time and took a nick out of my wrist.

"The rope, Jace, not the skin," I said through my teeth. I could feel warm blood trickling down my fingers and it was hard not to think about how slashing your wrists was such a popular way to kill yourself.

Jacey stopped slicing and sidewinder-slid herself around to stare into my face with those big, solemn eyes. "Am I hurting you real bad, Steve?"

"Naw," I lied gallantly, "you're not hurting me."

Jacey nodded with satisfaction. "I didn't think so. So would you just quit wiggling around and let me get this done?"

Several lacerations later I suddenly felt the rope go slack. Jacey the Ripper had done the job—and I was still alive. I flexed my aching hands a few times and then took the knife. "Here, Jace. I'll cut you loose."

She gave me a stern look over her shoulder. "Be careful you don't cut me."

Yeah, right.

Seconds later we were standing there, rubbing our wrists and looking for a way out. I checked my watch and had to look twice to believe my eyes. Nearly six o'clock. We'd been here for three hours. Enough time for Romero to drive from Calgary to Mountain Aire and for Russ Donovan and him to drive back here. We had to get out of here, *now*. That little window looked to be about the only chance, but it was way too small for me to fit. "Jace?" I said, looking up. "You figure you could get out that window?"

She gave it an appraising look. "Sure, *if* I could get up there."

I squatted down. "Get on my shoulders." She did and I maneuvered into position under the window.

"It won't open. I need something to break it with."

Moving carefully so I didn't dump her, I reached over and picked up a piece of firewood that seemed about right. I handed it up to her. Her weight shifted backward as she raised the wood above her head. Then her body whipped forward and the stick connected with the window. A gentle rain of sparkling glass fragments sifted through my hair and down my neck. So much for the window. "Can you climb out?" I asked.

Jacey inspected it. "Not without killin' myself. There's sharp pieces of glass stickin' out of the frame all over the place."

"Put my jacket over the worst of it," I said, working my way out of my jean jacket—which isn't easy with somebody sitting on your shoulders. I finally got it loose and handed it up to her.

"Here. Now be careful you don't fall."

"Stop givin' me advice or you can do this."

There was a lot of scrambling up there, for a second she was actually *standing* on my ear as if it was a rock ledge or something. Then all her weight was gone, and when I looked up, so was she. I held my breath, waiting for the thud and scream that would mean she'd fallen and broken her neck. There wasn't a sound. Then there was a rattle at the door. "Jacey? What's the deal? Is it padlocked?" If it was, it was going to be game over.

"No." Jacey's voice was strained and breathless. "It's just a latch but it's really stiff." More rattles. A few muffled words. Then, "Steve! I hear a car!"

I clenched my teeth to keep my voice level. "Never mind, Jace. Just concentrate on the door latch. You can get it. Do it, *now*."

"I'm trying but it won't—" There was a sudden squeal of metal and the door slammed back on its hinges. Jacey fell in behind it and landed in my arms.

I grabbed her hand and practically slingshot her out of there. "Run, Jace! Head for the car and don't look back!"

I pulled the shed door shut behind us and followed her across the parking lot toward the Charger. I got in just in time to see the black Jag skid into the driveway and come to a gravel-spraying stop. "Get down, Jace!" I yelled as I ducked as low as I could and reached for the key. It was there in the ignition, the best break we'd had all day. I used to be proud of how fast I could hot-wire, but it wouldn't have been fast enough to get us out of here alive.

As I turned the key I could see Romero and Donovan getting out in front of the shed. They thought we were still in there. A second later the engine caught and, at the sound, Romero spun around. There was a gun in his hand and he raised it to fire.

"Stay down, Jace!" I hollered and flattened myself along the seat. I'd never tried driving in that position before but it could be done. At least it could for the couple of seconds it took for a bullet to smash in through the back window and out through the windshield. Then the car was out on the road and a clump of trees cut off Romero's view. I sat up and gave her the gas. Gravel flew and the Charger's rear end whipped back and forth. I shifted up and she straightened out and flew. "Fasten your seat belt, Jace. This is gonna be a ride," I said, clicking my own belt.

Chapter 20

THE ROAD BEGAN TO CLIMB and twist and just as we clawed around the first curve I caught a glimpse of the Jag. It was on the road now and hot on our trail. So we were about to find out for once and for all if a North American gas-guzzler could outdo a European sports car. And the prize would be staying alive. We rounded the bend and the Jag disappeared. There was a straight, level stretch here so I put the spurs to Ol' Purple and asked her for everything she had. The engine roared and the needle climbed.

The road climbed again and I slapped that Hurst shifter into second and felt a surge of power as that big 440 engine turned loose the horses. All right! The Jag couldn't catch me on the upgrade—if I could hold the big old Charger on the road, that is. Rear wheels spinning, we slid around a hairpin curve in a four-wheel drift, and I felt the rear quarter-panel scrape along the rock wall on the inside. Better than going wide on the outside. The drop-off to the valley below was so deep it made the tops of the tall spruce down there look as smooth as a green velvet carpet.

I'd come close to buying it myself more times than I wanted to remember, but I'd never been this scared. This time, if I made one mistake, I was going to get my kid sister killed, and there wasn't a thing I could do about it except drive like I'd never driven in my life—and pray. If Romero caught up to us, this time I *would* be dead and he wouldn't be leaving a witness behind.

As I fought to hold the Charger on the road on yet another killer curve, something caught my eye. A narrow dirt side road that looked like it had only recently been slashed out of the timber cut off to my left. If I'd seen it in time I might have tried to disappear down there before Romero caught sight of me again. But it was too late—we were already past it. As the cutoff flashed by in a blur I caught a glimpse of something else—a loaded logging truck just laboring into sight, ready to turn onto the main road. If it had been a split second sooner...

I concentrated on the road. We were starting downhill again and I could see the Jag. It had gained a little. We rounded another bend and it disappeared from sight.

This downhill stretch was fairly straight and I was letting the Charger have her head. We were smokin' but I could see another curve coming up. No way could we make the turn at this speed. I'd just started to brake when I heard the bang. My first thought was that I'd blown a tire and we were toast, but in that same second I knew that wasn't it. The car didn't feel any different and the sound was wrong for a blowout. It sounded more like someone had set off a charge of dynamite. Then there was another bang, fainter and farther away. For the first time since we'd started this life-and-death car race, Jacey broke the silence in the car. "What was that?" she whispered.

"I don't know," I said, but actually I guess I did know—or at least I had a pretty good idea. A good enough idea that I started easing up on the gas and letting a little more speed bleed off. We made it around the curve and, when we hit another straight stretch, I watched in the mirror as I slowed a little more. Nothing. Finally, I braked to a full stop. We sat there for maybe five minutes while the adrenaline drained out of me enough so I could unclamp my hands from the wheel and take a few deep breaths. I was breathing like I'd run those last few miles on foot. "We've gotta go back," I said at last, glancing over at Jacey.

Her face was white and her eyes looked huge. I could see she was shaking but she nodded. "Okay, Steve," she said in a small voice.

I cranked the car around in the middle of the road and drove back up the twisting road. As I came around a hairpin bend just above the cutoff road I saw it. The logging truck was jackknifed across the road, completely blocking it. Its load had shifted and a few logs had come loose and were lying scattered, like some giant had spilled a handful of toothpicks. One front fender of the big rig was crumpled and a headlight was broken, but that was all the damage I could see.

The driver was standing on the road holding a handkerchief over a cut on his forehead and shaking his head as he stared out over the sheer drop off to the valley below. "Stay here, Jace," I said as I got out and walked over to him. He didn't seem to be hurt much, but he was pretty shook.

"Crazy fool came around that corner in the middle of the road doing about ninety miles an hour. I tried to pull over but there was nowhere to go. I just about rolled the rig tryin' to miss him. It was no use. That little sports car just crumpled up like a piece of newspaper. I'd bet both the guys in it were dead before they went over. If they weren't, they are now. She blew when she hit the bottom."

"I'll say she blew." Jacey's voice cut in from right beside me, where I might have known she'd be in spite of my orders. For a minute we all just stood there, looking down at the bright orange flames and the column of black smoke. That was all there was. The black Jag—and Romero and Donovan—were history.

The truck driver took a cell phone out of his pocket, turned it on, and hit three buttons. He waited a minute, shook his head, and turned it off. "No signal here," he said. "And the crash must've shook somethin' loose on the CB. I already tried it. We need to get some cops up here."

Right, I thought, just what we need. "If you'll be okay here for a while, we'll go back to Mountain Aire and call from there," I said.

"Yeah, I'm okay, but you'll have to go on up to Nordegg instead. My rig's blockin' the road to Mountain Aire."

"Okay, hang in there. I'll tell them to hurry. Let's go, Jace." I turned the car around again. I was getting good at doing it with the Charger's back end bumping the rock wall and the front end hanging out over eternity. I got straightened out and pointed her north. Mile after mile slid by with no sound but the contented purr of a motor that had let all those horses under the hood get out and run for a change. I'd have never believed that listening to Jacey say absolutely nothing could be so hard to take.

Finally, I couldn't take it any longer. "Talk to me, Jace."

She turned to look at me, all huge, dark eyes in a white face. "What do you want me to say?" she asked in a voice that didn't sound like her.

I let out a deep breath. "Oh, I dunno, Jace. How about something like, 'You idiot! What was that all about? Where do you get off almost gettin' me killed because of something that started years ago and didn't have anything to do with me?'"

A little spark came back into her eyes. "Okay," she said, her voice toughening up a little. "So maybe *you* better talk to *me*, Steve."

So I talked. I talked all the way to Nordegg. I told my ten-year-old sister more than I'd ever told anyone else about being a street kid in Vancouver who got mixed up with Carlos Romero's drug dealing business. I told her about how much I had loved Tracey and how—while I was in jail and Romero was supposed to be looking out for her—he got her into cocaine and how she overdosed and died. How, when I found out she was dead, I walked away from day parole and swore to make Romero pay. How, only knowing that Tracey's memory deserved better kept me from trying to kill him. How, instead, I'd tipped off Crime Stoppers about where to catch him collecting a new drug shipment. How, with the kind of lawyers his dirty money could buy, he got off.

Jacey listened for an hour without a single interruption, but with Nordegg coming into sight she took over and finished the story. "And he's been after you ever since, and that's why there's all this mystery about why you were in Montana and why it was so hard to find you and everything?"

Obviously Jacey had listened in on a few conversations with me as the main topic. I nodded. "You got it, kid."

She thought for a minute. "And you couldn't report him to the police because you're a wanted man in the eyes of the law."

I couldn't help but smile at the way she put that. I figured she must have watched one too many old western movies but she was still right on. "Right again, Jace."

There was a long silence. Then, "Gee, Steve, you really messed up big time."

And that pretty much summed up my life so far.

Chapter 21

IT WAS ALMOST DARK when we drove up to the gas station, which made up most of the town of Nordegg these days. It was a big mining town once but the mines closed fifty years ago and now it's mostly a ghost town. There was a pay phone outside the gas station and I made another of my trademark anonymous calls. When the 911 operator answered I said, "There's been a bad wreck just south of Ram Falls on the Forestry Trunk Road. A car with two people in it hit a logging truck head-on and went over a hundred-foot drop-off and exploded. The truck driver has minor injuries. You need to send whatever it takes to get the jackknifed logging truck off the road and the spilled logs picked up." I said it all in one breath, ignoring the operator's voice as she tried to break in with questions.

She was still trying when I finished. "What is your name? Are you at the scene now?"

I hung up and got back in the car.

I drove slow all the way down Highway 11 to Rocky Mountain House. That country was full of game and speeding over a hill to come face to face with a big dark shape and eyes shining in the headlights was the last surprise I needed tonight. Now that the adrenaline rush of that wild drive had worn off, I was so tired I could hardly keep my eyes open. I figured Jacey *was* asleep— all curled up in the corner, looking young and innocent. She didn't look like someone who had come real close to getting killed this afternoon. But just as my conscience was giving me another working over on that subject, she sat up straight and looked at me. "Steve?"

"Yeah?"

"It's gonna work out all right. Don't worry."

"Except for the fact that I messed up big time, you mean?"

"Well, everybody should get a second chance. I'm not mad at you anymore." She paused and thought a minute. "But I betcha Mom will be."

"No kiddin'."

It was just after midnight when I drove into Pop's yard. I had a headache from getting hit with the tire iron—and all the car headlights we met multiplying into a few hundred blinding stars by the cracks around the bullet hole in the windshield didn't help any. But I knew I was soon going to feel a whole lot worse. The yard light was on. The porch light was on. Every light in the house was on. And Mom and Pop were both out on the front porch. For a minute all I could think of was that this must be what it would have been like if I'd been a normal kid in a normal family and I'd stayed out too late. But then I remembered that neither I nor my family had been exactly normal for a real long time and that, instead of hangin' out with my buddies too long, I'd spent the afternoon coming within a hair of getting both myself and my ten-year-old sister killed. I was going to have some explaining to do.

Jacey and I got out of the car. Before Jacey got her door shut Mom was there, wrapping her arms around her and asking was she okay and what had happened and never letting her get enough air to answer any of those questions. Meanwhile, Pop came ambling over, studied the situation, and stuck a finger through the hole in the windshield. He cocked his head in my direction and gave me a questioning look. But, before I could say anything, Mom gave up on squashing Jacey, took one look at that windshield, and turned on me.

I thought she was going to start screaming at me and blaming me for putting Jacey in danger and I knew that this time I wouldn't fight back. She couldn't say anything to make me feel any worse than I already did. Every time I thought about how close I came to getting Jacey killed, I felt sick.

"Steve..." she began but then she reached out toward me and I took half a step backward. I was sure she was going to actually light into me with her fists. But the next thing I knew she had her arms around me, and she was crying into my shoulder and trying to talk between sobs. "Steve, I am so sorry. Your dad just told me about Romero and how Russ Donovan had teamed up with him after you fought him and took Spook away from him. Donovan was *here*, Steve. He came to the door looking for you a couple of days ago, and I practically welcomed him with open arms. And then he came back this afternoon. Nobody else was here but I'd read Jacey's note saying you'd headed for Ram Falls so I *told* him. Whatever happened up there, it's my fault. It's all my fault. Steve, can you forgive me...for everything?" She stopped talking, dragged in a couple of ragged breaths, then raised her head and gave me a searching look. "I couldn't stand to lose you again, Steve."

Again? I thought, and then what Beau had told me earlier came flooding back into my mind. This wasn't turning out exactly the way I'd expected. For a minute, I just stood there with her arms around me, tense as a wild colt the first time he's touched by a human. And, then I felt myself slowly begin to relax. This wasn't so bad. Maybe I could learn to live with it.

Slowly my arms reached out to hold my mom. "It's okay, Mom," I said. "We were in big trouble but Jacey came through. Didn't you, Jace?"

"Well," said Jacey, who I could see had enjoyed about all this sloppy stuff that she could stand. "I *was* the only one with sense enough to bring my knife. But never mind that right now. I'm starving."

A couple of days later I got a message from Beau. Basically it said, *Get in here. I want to talk to you.* So, I went.

He was lying real still, propped up against the pillows and looking about as limp as a sick kitten. White-on-white was the best way I could describe his face against the pillow. But the minute I walked in I could see he had something on his mind.

"Hey, Beau," I said, pasting on a stupid grin like I thought you were supposed to have when visiting in the hospital.

"Hey," he said, his voice weak. He didn't bother trying to dredge up a phony grin of his own. He just reached over to the bedside table, picked up a newspaper, and handed it to me. It was folded open to a page somewhere in the middle. I scanned the headlines and settled on:

RCMP INVESTIGATING FATAL CRASH ON FORESTRY ROAD

Two unidentified men died in a fiery crash on the Forestry Trunk Road near Ram River Falls on Tuesday. Their B.C.-registered Jaguar was apparently traveling north on the twisting mountain road at a high rate of speed when it was involved in a collision with a logging truck. Out of control, the car then went off the road and exploded on impact at the bottom of a fifty-meter drop-off. The driver of the logging truck sustained only minor injuries. Police are investigating but say it is unlikely that charges will be laid against the truck driver. They are seeking the two occupants of what the truck driver described as "a purple muscle car" who may have been witnesses to events leading up to the crash.

Beau's eyes burned dark in his pale face as he gave me a searching look and asked a one-word question. "Romero?"

"Yeah," was the one-word answer.

Beau sighed and closed his eyes for a minute. His breathing sounded loud and strained in the silent room. Then he looked at me again. "So it's over now?" he asked, almost in a whisper.

Was it over?

"I don't know, Beau. I guess that part's over. With Romero and me it was personal. None of his hired guns are gonna come lookin' for me now. So, yeah, it's over. Except that I'm still officially an escaped convict. The cops ever happen to run across me, I'll still go to jail. So that part's not over."

"You could make it be over, Steve. It's time it was over." His voice trailed off into nothing and his eyes closed.

I thought he'd gone to sleep but a minute later his eyes opened again. "So," he said, about as defiantly as anybody without the energy to get above a whisper could, "what are you gonna do now? Just ride off into the sunset again and spend the rest of your life sneakin' around like a weasel?"

I didn't think that was a very respectful way to talk to somebody whose stem cells were setting up shop in your body to keep you alive. But Beau was definitely not in a good mood.

Since I couldn't slug somebody in his condition I just shrugged. "I dunno what I'm gonna do. Stick around here until you're back on your feet and then figure something out."

He gave me a look that said that wasn't the right answer. "Or you could turn yourself in to the cops, do whatever you have to do to settle that old parole violation, then start livin' a normal life that doesn't include lookin' over your shoulder all the time."

I shook my head. "I don't know, Beau. Maybe I've been lookin' over my shoulder too long to stop. I can't even remember what a normal life feels like any more. I think, when you get better, it might be time for me to hit the road again. See you later, kid," I said, standing up to leave before he got on my case about anything else.

"Yeah, maybe you better run." Beau's voice was quiet but with a knife-edge to it. "You've still got at least one person on your trail."

That stopped me in my tracks. "What?"

Beau managed a tired "gotcha" grin. "Yeah, she phoned here last fall wonderin' if we knew where you were."

I fought back an urge to grab my brother by the throat and shake him. "*Who* phoned here lookin' for me?"

Beau took his own sweet time answering. "I think she said her name was Lynne."

"*Lynne* phoned here lookin' for me?"

"Is there an echo in here? Isn't that what I just said?"

"How'd she know to phone here?" I asked, sounding about as stunned as I felt.

Beau shrugged. "How should I know? I suppose you must have told her we lived at Fenton. From there on it's not hard. Pop's number's in the book."

"So what did you tell her? About where I was, I mean."

"The truth. That you were someplace in the States and we didn't know where." He paused and then added. "She sounded real disappointed."

I stared at him, trying to gauge whether he'd added that part just to rattle my chain a little.

But his face was dead serious. "Where was she callin' from?" I asked.

Another shrug. "She didn't say and I didn't ask. Since nobody knew where you were, it didn't seem to much matter where she was." Beau shifted restlessly on the pillow. "But I bet you could find her if you wanted to bad enough."

I didn't say anything. My mind was somewhere far away, remembering the good times.

She said that in her goodbye letter back at Rock Creek. Remember the good times. That's when she'd left me with nothing but a little gold Camaro to remember *her* by. I'd thought I'd never see her again after that, but we did meet again—at the Calgary Stampede—and this time we almost made it. We drove out of there together, headed for the border. But I was the one who said goodbye that time. I realized I couldn't take a girl like Lynne into the kind of world I was living in. I made her go back.

When I closed my eyes the picture of Lynne I always saw was her crying through the rain-streaked window of a Greyhound bus. Lynne was about the best thing that ever happened to me, and all I ever did was hurt her. But there was no way I ever planned to see her crying over me again.

"So, do you?" Beau's voice dragged me back to the hospital room.

"Do I what?"

"Want to find her bad enough?"

I shook my head and swallowed hard but my voice still came out kind of ragged. "No," I lied. "Lynne and I are ancient history. It's over. Let it go, Beau," I said. "I don't need any help sorting out my love life."

"Could've fooled me," he muttered as I turned and headed for the door.

Then I remembered something I'd been meaning to tell him before he got on my case about Lynne. "Hey," I said, over my shoulder. "Mom's waitin' to see you. She and I drove in together."

Beau's eyes opened wide, and something that almost passed for a grin crossed his face. "Well," he said with a sigh. "At least that's something."

Days passed. I was so on edge that I jumped every time the phone rang. But no call came from the cops inquiring about my "purple muscle car." The Charger had been back in the garage and out of sight ever since we came back from Ram Falls, and I was guessing that nobody I'd met coming back in the dark that night had noticed my shattered windshield. Then, one day there was another small item in the paper.

Accident victim identified as B.C. drug dealer

Police have released the names of the two men who died in the fiery crash on the Forestry Trunk Road last week. The driver was identified as Carlos Romero, 38, of Vancouver, a person well known to Vancouver police for his role in the importation and distribution of cocaine and other illegal substances. He had been arrested on several occasions but never convicted. His companion was Russell Donovan, 34, formerly of the Fenton, Alberta area and also a person of interest to the police. The driver of the logging truck, which was in the collision with Romero's late model Jaguar, has been exonerated of all wrongdoing. The RCMP report that the case is officially closed.

In other words, the police were unofficially saying, "It couldn't have happened to a nicer pair of guys. Let's move on."

So I was off the hook, as far as that whole business was concerned. But there was still the little matter of my parole violation. I had walked away from day parole back in Vancouver when Tracey died. I'd still be looking over my shoulder until I turned myself in and did my time—or whatever it was the law wanted of me. I couldn't bring myself to take that step yet. I needed a better reason than I had right now.

Chapter 22

IT WASN'T TOO LONG AFTER that when Beau started to get a little better. All the tests were showing that his body was accepting the transplant. But he had been so sick for so many months that it was going to be a long slow road back. Everybody knew that but him. A little over a month after the transplant he wrote his grade twelve final exams—in the hospital with Raine's mother as official supervisor. I couldn't believe he'd even wanted to try. He'd missed a bunch of school and was still in kind of rough shape, but he wanted to do it. Raine's mom said half his mark would come from his year's work, and that part would be really good. He'd do anything to keep from letting it show—and I'd do anything to keep from admitting it to his face—but my brother is a pretty smart kid. He'd made up his mind he was not only going to pass grade twelve but he was going to graduate with his class. I found that out the day he asked what the date was.

I had to think a minute. " June sixth, I think. Why?"

"Just wondered how long it was till grad. I've got almost a month."

I gave him a puzzled look. "What do you mean, you've got almost a month?"

He shook his head at my cluelessness. "To get sprung from this joint so I can go, of course."

"Hey, Beau, I don't think so. You know what the doctor told you before the transplant. It'll probably be nearly three months before you've got enough immunity built up to go out in the germs again. And," I added, trying to lighten things up a little, "I can't think of anything germier than a bunch of high school kids."

Beau totally ignored that line and just gave me a level look. "I worked for twelve years to get out of school and I'm goin' out in a blaze of glory like everybody else."

"Yeah," I muttered. "You go and catch somethin' deadly and you'll go out in a blaze of glory all right."

Beau gave an impatient sigh. "Steve, lately I've had more parents lookin' after me than I've had for most of my life. I don't need a third one. Get back to bein' my crazy, live-fast, love-hard, die-young brother or get outta here." He paused. "Besides, Raine's the valedictorian and I've gotta be there to hear her speech. And," there was another pause. Then he added very seriously, "She's actually gonna wear a DRESS. *That* I've gotta see."

"Well," I said, copying his serious tone, "maybe I could just look at her twice as hard for you. Wouldn't that work?"

He threw his water jug at me, and I got out of there before his large and scary nurse blamed me for it.

Two days before grad Dr. Addersly reluctantly let Beau go home. He was still a long ways from healthy but she said that, either because of or in spite of the fact that he was as stubborn as a mule in mud, he was making one of the fastest recoveries of any patient she'd ever had. He'd made up his mind he was going, and she figured it was easier to send him out the front door than to keep an armed guard at the back door. And, since he was eighteen, there wasn't anything Pop or Mom could do to keep him in there any longer.

So he came home, said hi to the horses, and then fell into bed, too tired to do anything but read, sleep, and play "pounce on the covers" with Willie—who had apparently decided he would rather be a nurse than a hunter.

But on the morning of grad Beau was wide-awake and bossy as all get-out. "If you're comin' to my grad, you better get yourself some formal clothes," he said sternly, watching me dress in a holey t-shirt and a pair of old jeans. "Don't want people thinkin' the Garretts ain't civilized."

"I can't think where they'd get that idea," I said.

So that afternoon I bought myself a new pair of black jeans and a white shirt. That was about as formal as I planned on getting—and also as far as I could stretch the last of my Cadillac Ranch money. I'd have just enough left for a trip to the barber and one more item I was going to need.

Beau was asleep when I got home so I just stayed out of his way until it was time to go.

I had to smile when he came downstairs. He was wearing black jeans and a white shirt, too. We Garrett boys definitely have the same fine fashion sense.

He looked me over. "What's got into you?" he asked.

"What do you mean? Don't I look all right?"

"The hat, genius. You never wear a Stetson. You look like a kid playing cowboy."

I shrugged. "Thanks a lot," I said. "I thought you looked great in yours so I decided to give it a try. Do I really look that bad?"

It was Beau's turn to shrug. "Naw, not that bad. Just weird."

With that vote of confidence we headed out to pick up Raine. I would've liked to take the Charger, but it was still laid up in Pop's garage recovering from its bullet wound. Instead, I got to drive Beau's truck. Beau still wasn't up to driving so I was invited along as chauffeur. Mom, Pop and Jacey were coming in Mom's car.

When the gorgeous blonde in the blue dress came out of Raine's house I almost didn't recognize her. "Wow!" I said as she got in the truck.

"Shut up, Steve," she said. Beau didn't say anything. He just put his arm around her and smiled.

The three of us stepped into the high school gym and all froze in the doorway. This didn't look like any gym I remembered. All the walls were covered in black paper and studded with hundreds of little tinfoil stars that glowed in the light of about a million tiny white Christmas lights. Silver and blue streamers looped and twisted from the ceiling, and across the front of the stage huge silver letters spelled out FOLLOW YOUR STAR. "Awesome!" Raine whispered, and for a minute there I thought she was going to cry. I wouldn't go that far but I had to admit that somebody had done a pretty fine job on the place.

Then some kid yelled, "Hey! There's Beau!" and a minute later a dozen of his friends surrounded him. I was beginning to understand how special this night was for him.

A few minutes later the chaos was roughly under control. We all sat down and the MC welcomed everybody and went through all the usual stuff to begin a ceremony. Then he said, "Please stand for the singing of O Canada." I felt Beau stiffen beside me. I knew how bad he was going to hate this. He'd been wearing the Stetson or a ball cap whenever he made it to school up until he went into the hospital. Everybody knew why and nobody gave him static about it. But that was different from having everybody looking at him and seeing what an eighteen-year-old bald guy looked like. He could have left the hat on. Nobody would have said anything. But Beau couldn't do that either. You always took your hat off for the national anthem, and he didn't want any special treatment. Reluctantly, he reached up and pulled his hat off. I did the same.

It was Raine who noticed first. She was sitting on the stage facing the audience, waiting to give her valedictorian's speech. I saw her mouth fall open. She gave kind of a gasp, and then she covered her mouth with her hand but the rest of her face was laughing. Then Pop looked at me. He raised one eyebrow in his patented "Pop look" and reached over and gave my shoulder a squeeze. That little commotion caught Mom's attention and, from over on the other side of Beau she turned to look at me. She started to cry. *That* really got Jacey's attention. She turned to have a really good gawk. "C-o-o-l!" she said in a voice that carried above the singing. *That* got *everybody's* attention, and a couple of hundred heads turned in our direction.

I think Beau was the last one in the building to notice. He'd been staring at the floor. He finally glanced in my direction, stared like he was seeing an extra-terrestrial, and for a minute there I was afraid he was going to pass out. Then he started to laugh.

"O Canada" limped to a feeble end as that whole gym full of people suddenly broke into applause. I don't think it was because they were feeling patriotic. They were all looking at the two totally bald Garrett boys, who were standing there with their arms around each other and laughing their heads off.

As the applause died down, there was a sudden silence. "It must be a genetic defect," some old lady on the other side of the room said in one of those out-loud whispers. We just laughed harder.

When the audience finally settled down there was some of the usual grad-type chit-chat from the stage—at least I guess it was the usual; this was the closest to graduating I'd ever come. The principal made one of those principal-type speeches about what fine, upstanding young people these kids were and how the school wouldn't be the same without them. If this guy was anything like the last couple of principals I'd met in my short and eventful school career, what he really meant was, "Thank God I've survived to see them go."

Chapter 23

THEN IT WAS TIME FOR RAINE'S SPEECH. She walked to the podium and stood there looking out at the audience for a minute. She was so beautiful in that dress. It was made of some kind of shiny stuff in that exact shade of thundercloud blue her eyes always got when she was about to tear a strip off you for something.

I can't remember too much of what she said. It was on the same theme as the decorations, all about following your star and not letting anything stop you from going after what you want in life. But I do remember what she said at the end. "And when you've faced the hardest thing that life can throw at you and you've walked through fire and kept going and come out the other side, stronger and better than ever, then you haven't just followed your star. You *are* a star, and you always will be." She looked right into Beau's eyes and I saw the way he was looking at her. Maybe they were just a couple of kids, but I knew right then that they belonged together.

She'd always be special to me but she'd always be Beau's girl.

Then some other guy made a fairly dry speech and then everybody got their diplomas and threw their hats in the air. Beau had officially graduated right there with the rest of his class. He was looking pretty tired, and I heard Mom ask him if he was ready to go home yet. He shook his head, and he and Raine found a spot on the sidelines as the DJ set up for the dance. I thought it might be about time for me to split, but since nobody else in my family seemed about to leave and I didn't have any transportation, I just leaned against the wall and watched the dance.

At least I planned to watch but apparently bald must be beautiful. Girls started coming up and asking me to dance with them. I did and it was okay, even kind of fun, pretending I had actually made it through high school and this was my graduation.

But as it got later and the music slowed down, I started to feel seriously out of place. This wasn't my life I was living here. I didn't belong. These were kids with a future, kids who knew where they were going. All I had was a past, and I didn't really want to think about where I'd been. I was dancing with one of Raine's friends now. She was pretty and funny and I could tell she liked me. Don't ask me how it's possible to be dancing with a gorgeous seventeen-year-old girl and be feeling lonely as hell but it is. Because I was.

There were only three girls I'd ever really cared about. Tracey was dead, Raine was in love with my brother, and Lynne—well, I didn't know where Lynne was now. We fell in love but broke up twice because I couldn't shake the shadow Romero threw over my life. Now Romero was gone but, as far as I was concerned, Lynne was too. I couldn't ask her to try a third time.

The dance ended and Raine's friend went off to dance with some other guy. Then the DJs voice cut in above the music. "Okay, boys and girls, time to find the love of your life. Here comes the last dance." His voice faded out and was replaced by some slow and romantic song.

Raine and Beau had been sitting on one of the benches along the side of the gym for most of the evening. Now Beau stood up and held his hand out to Raine. Holding hands, they walked out onto the crowded dance floor. Beau looked pretty pale and shaky but he wasn't about to fall over—Raine was holding him too close for that. They looked great together. Just watching them, I knew Beau was going to be all right now. It was the best moment since I'd stood in that phone booth in Butte and felt my world fall apart. So what was wrong with me? Why did I suddenly feel more alone than I'd ever felt on the streets or in jail or hiding out a thousand miles from home?

It was getting hot in the gym and I was beginning to feel like all those people were closing in on me. I needed to get out of there. I walked over to where the open door let in the cool night air and just stood there, staring up at the black, star-studded sky.

I could smell wildflowers. That was pretty strange since the door opened onto a parking lot full of exhaust fumes. That smell took me back to last summer—to the last time I'd been back in Alberta. That was when Lynne had found me at the Calgary Stampede, took me up on the Ferris wheel and wouldn't let me down until I admitted I wasn't mad at her for leaving me a "Dear John" letter and disappearing the year before. Her hair had smelled like wildflowers when I kissed her at the top of the Ferris wheel and the first fireworks went off. But then Romero had showed up and everything had changed...

"I sure like what you've done with your hair, cowboy," a voice behind me said. I turned around. I'd quit the dope a long time ago, but for a minute there I felt like I must be high again. I was seeing things that weren't there.

"Are you real?" I said softly, as I turned to look into Lynne's dark eyes. "You can't be here. You don't even know I'm here."

She laughed. "Come on. Let's dance," she said as she took my hand and led me to a space on the crowded floor. "Beau made me come. He phoned me a month ago and said you'd come back here and saved his life, and the only way he could think of to save yours was to find me."

"Beau? He was in the hospital three-quarters dead a month ago."

"I know. But the quarter that was alive was on the phone tracking me down. When I answered the phone he sounded like a real old lady. I thought it was my ninety-four-year-old great-great-aunt. You can imagine he wasn't too impressed when I said, 'Oh hi, Aunt Nellie. How are you doin'?'"

"So how'd he find you?"

"It wasn't so hard. I'm back at Rock Creek staying with Carl and Connie and teaching high school again."

"No kiddin'? I thought you'd enjoyed about all the teachin' you could stand after that first year."

"Well, I learned a lot that year and started off a little older and wiser this time. I lived to even see your friend Mitch graduate. Tonight was Grad there, too. I had to at least put in an appearance, so that's why I'm so late getting here." She looked up at me with a dangerous grin. "Some of the wildest kids have improved their behavior a lot because of a rumor going around school that I had this real tough outlaw boyfriend."

"Wonder where they got that idea?"

"Steve, would you just shut up and pay attention? You're standing on my foot."

But I was kind of distracted just then because I'd looked across the gym and could hardly believe my eyes. Mom and Pop were out there dancing together—and they actually looked like they might know what they were doing. This was turning out to be some romantic kind of night for the Garretts. Even Jacey had found a friend. She and some little dude with red hair that mostly stood straight up were busy tearing up paper cups to make boats with toothpick masts, and sailing them across the punch bowl.

I closed my eyes then and listened to the music and held Lynne. For a little while there, I didn't worry about tomorrow. Then the song ended and I came back to reality. For a minute Lynne and I just stood there, studying each other's faces in the dim glow of those hundreds of tiny fake stars on the ceiling.

Finally she broke the silence. "So, where do we go from here, Steve?"

I thought about just saying "Home," but I knew she was waiting for a real answer—one I wasn't sure I had. "It's not gonna work, Lynne," I said, my voice coming out kind of ragged. "My life is still messed up pretty bad. I'm probably gonna end up doin' jail time before I ever get my past straightened out. You don't want to be tangled up with somebody like me. You'll just get hurt."

She shook her head. "You just don't get it, do you Steve? I *am* tangled up with you. You think I drove halfway across Alberta tonight to say goodbye again? The only way you can hurt me is to shut me out of your life. Don't do that to me again, Steve." She stood there, looking up at me and burning a hole in my heart with those dark eyes.

I took a deep breath and surrendered. I reached for her hand and we walked outside into the light of the real stars. One star was brighter than all the others.

"See that star over there?" I said at last. "Want to follow it with me?"